Urgently R

RACHEL RAFFERTY

CW01432063

Urgently Required

Published by Rachel Rafferty 2023

Copyright © 2023 Rachel Rafferty

All rights reserved.

This is a work of fiction. Characters, names, places, brands, media, incidents and events portrayed in this book are fictitious. Any similarity to real persons, living or dead, is unintentional and co-incidental.

No part of this publication may be reproduced, stored in a retrieval system, or transmitted in any form or by any means, electronic, mechanical, photocopying, recording or otherwise, without the prior written permission from both the copyright owner and publisher.

Visit: Rachelrafferty.com

'This Is To Mother You'

Sinéad O'Connor
(Gospel Oak)

Prologue

When I was twelve, I distinctly remember I wanted them to break up. It was when she threw a loaf of bread at him. It didn't hurt in the slightest, only a Brennan's whole grain loaf it was. The packaging ripped on impact and my mother cursed the fact that now the bread wouldn't keep. He was in a state of shock, not really registering what it was that hit him on the head. I thanked God he only made a mistake with the bread. If he'd bought the wrong brand of beans, then who knows? Maybe a tin of beans hurled to his head would have knocked him out.

I wasn't really sure what to do. My mother kicked the loaf to the corner, muttering that she'd wanted wholemeal, not wholegrain, and left the kitchen. Dad rubbed his forehead. I picked up the sliced loaf, sellotaped the packaging and put it in the breadbin. Surely, myself or Dad or my younger brother, Alan, would eat it. We had no such preferences when it came to bread. There wasn't much difference once it was toasted, buttered and dolloped with raspberry jam.

I looked at Dad. He still looked as if he was in a state of shock following the blow. I offered him a tissue. I don't know why. He wasn't bleeding or anything, but that's all I did. That's what a terrible daughter I was. He stood there in the kitchen, rubbing his head while staring into space, and all I did was offer him a tissue.

He never complained. I thought he would after that. I thought maybe that would have been the last straw, but he recovered when my mother returned to the kitchen. Nothing more was said about it. The next morning, I noticed a loaf of wholemeal in the breadbin. The wholegrain was gone. I was kind of looking forward to trying some new bread, but I couldn't find it. We all had toasted wholemeal as usual for breakfast and my dad never bought the wrong bread again.

I don't have many more vivid memories of my dad, apart from the daily bickering and yelling he engaged in with my mother. As I knelt by his grave, my mother rattled off some prayers she knew by heart and I thought about the tissue I'd offered him when I was twelve. Did he use it? Was it even clean? I think I pulled it out from up my sleeve. It could have been one I'd used already. I put my head down. 'Sorry Daddy,' I muttered under my breath. I didn't want my mother to hear me apologising. 'I'm so sorry,' I whispered.

Chapter One

'You look pale,' my mother alerted me.

'Oh? I put a bit of makeup on earlier and…'

'Hmm, very washed out. You need a tonic or something. You're not well,' she insisted.

'Oh, I feel fine. I went for a walk this morning and…'

'Get yourself an iron supplement. That might be what's wrong with you.'

I pulled my little notebook out of my bag. Yes, I was a list maker. I'd never remember to do anything otherwise. I wrote 'Tuesday, 27th Jan - Chemist : Get iron supplement or tonic.'

'Consider it done!' I smiled at my mother. She didn't smile back, but I knew she had my best interests at heart. I mean, maybe I was a bit run-down, what with it being a desperately cold January and all the bugs flying around the library currently. Half the staff were on sick leave. I was doing extra shifts to cover for them. Mother was right. I needed a tonic to keep my energy levels up. I felt them dipping just thinking about it. Yes, some sort of supplement was urgently required. She was right.

We carried on shopping until she'd crossed everything off her list and then I drove her to the chiropodist. She had a car of her own but tended to be a nervous driver, so whenever I had a day off I taxied her around in my trusty Renault Clio.

'Your car's filthy, Emma. I'd be embarrassed if the chiropodist saw me getting out of it. Park around the corner and I'll hobble the rest of the way.'

I did as requested. I didn't think my car was too bad, although I had recently come back from a weekend away with the girls. We went on a shopping trip to Belfast to check out the January sales. I did the driving, even though, technically, it wasn't my turn. It was Julia's, but she was afraid to bring her brand new Fiesta up north, so I volunteered. Well, not so much volunteered, I suppose. I was nominated by Helen. She thought there would be more room in my Clio than her Toyota Yaris. I was doubtful, but didn't want to argue, so I picked them up and drove. The weather was diabolical, so I suppose maybe the car did get dirty. I hadn't gotten around to getting it cleaned since the trip.

I'd driven a lot during that weekend. Our hotel was miles outside town, so I was the designated driver for our two nights out. I would have liked to have had a drink with dinner on at least one of the nights, but Julia didn't want to have dinner in the hotel or the surroundings. She wanted to get into the city centre as there was a buzz about town. She was trying to meet someone. We all were, but Julia seemed to be in more of a hurry than myself and Helen. She was right—there seemed to be plenty of single men in the bars of Belfast and we got talking to a few potentials. Well, I didn't say much. I let the girls do the talking. They had plenty of Dutch courage due to the cocktails they'd consumed after dinner. My sparkling water didn't exactly make me sparkle.

They all seemed drunk and I was getting tired. We stayed out late, until the clubs ended and I drove them back to the hotel, both of them stocious and still single. The next day I was glad I had no hangover. It was a long journey home and the girls slept so I needed to be alert for driving. Yeah, it was a good weekend. I bought a skirt and boots for work. I didn't think they were any cheaper than what you'd get in Dublin though, so I wouldn't exactly be rushing back to Belfast for the bargains.

I got a fright when my mother tapped on the window. Oh gosh, forty-five minutes had passed and I'd just been sitting in the car in dreamland. I got out to help her into the passenger seat.

'The least you could have done was to pull around. I had to hobble around the corner with excruciating pain in my left foot.' She wasn't happy.

'Oh, but you said my car was dirty. I was saving you the embarrassment of…'

'You could have pulled up nearby and waited until you saw the door close. Then, you could have come closer when the chiropodist turned away.'

'Okay, well, I'll do that next time. So, where to next? Or will I drop you home now?' I asked, hoping she'd choose the latter, but unfortunately for me, she wanted to call over to a friend who had lost her husband recently. I really had wanted to get home and see what Helen and Julia were up to but when I heard it was Bernadette we were calling to, I cheered up a bit. I really liked Bernadette. She was always so cheerful and bright. How she was friendly with my mother, I couldn't fathom, but maybe it was true what they said—opposites attract.

*   *   *

We left Bernadette's later that afternoon with a bag of homemade buns each. Bernadette was a baker and she insisted on sharing her goods. She was such a kind lady and seemed to be coping quite well after the death of her beloved husband, Roger. She shed a tear or two when she mentioned him. I marvelled when she did. I never thought to do that when my father's name was mentioned in passing. Tears just didn't come to my eyes when I was reminded of his death. My mother was the very same. I'd never seen her cry, not even at the funeral.

Maybe we were cut from the same cloth. I shuddered at the thought.

It was late when I got home. Julia and Helen were already in the city centre. They encouraged me to come and join them but it was already eight o'clock and I was tired. I didn't feel like I was going to meet the man of my dreams tonight so I declined. The three of us were in our mid to late thirties and beyond ready to settle down. We often had a laugh wondering which of us would meet someone first. Helen was definitely the prettiest so we imagined it would be her, although Julia was tall with long hair and shapely legs so it was a tough call. None of us thought it would be me. I understood. I was neither the slimmest nor the most fashionable. I was a librarian and tended to dress like one, even out of hours. Comfort was key and I couldn't get away from that fact, even on a Saturday night out in Dublin.

I actually wasn't sure if I'd meet my future husband on a drunken night out on the town. After two to three drinks I'd normally get tired and slip away home, leaving the girls to go clubbing. Mother usually needed me to bring her to mass and then the graveyard on Sunday morning anyways, so I was always glad when I arrived home before midnight.

*   *   *

'I'm mortified. Look at the state of the plants. Two are overturned. I hope Bernadette wasn't visiting Roger's grave and noticed this mess. Mortified, I am.'

Mother was mortified about the state of Dad's grave. I didn't think it looked too bad. The wind had blown over a plant or two but it was January, so that was to be expected. I doubted Bernadette would be judgmental about that kind of thing but I thought it better not to pass comment either way. I picked up the plants and pulled some long grass around the gravestone.

I thought I'd have the afternoon to myself after that. I wanted to use the new mini power steamer I'd bought for my bathroom. The tiles were looking a bit grimy of late, so I was hoping to freshen them up. However, my mother wanted me to pull some weeds in her cobblelock driveway. She was right. The recent rainfall had lured them out of hiding. I asked her when she last saw Alan.

'He came over last night with Sophie, the new girlfriend.'

'Oh? What's she like?' I hadn't met her yet, but Alan seemed to have a new girlfriend every month, so it was impossible to keep up.

'Her mother's a lawyer and father's a banker, very high up,' my mother informed me.

'I see, but what's she like?' I asked.

'A bit full of herself. She has a pointy nose,' she answered.

'Does Alan seem keen?' I wondered if he'd settle down before me. There was only three years between us. I imagined he probably would, since he nearly always had a girlfriend on the go and I was, for the most part, single.

'No keener than on any other of his lady friends. He's keen to go on holiday to Greece with her and her parents, though. All expenses paid for a week in a beach villa. What d'you think of that?' she asked with raised eyebrows.

'Wow! He's landed on his feet with her. Sounds like a real catch!' I replied, matching her sense of awe. But does he like her? I still wondered. I'd have to ask him. That sort of thing didn't seem to interest my mother.

'Did he notice the weeds were a bit overgrown while he was here?' I enquired.

'Oh, yes, he mentioned something about it, but I reassured him you'd be over at the weekend to pull them.'

'Oh, I see. It's just that I did it the last time, before Christmas, and we both agreed it would be his turn next time.'

'There were hardly any visible last time. Negligible, it was.' She waved her hand in the air.

I thought about it. I suppose it didn't take me long to clear them the last time. She was right.

There weren't many. That said, I had done a massive haul the month before, thinking that would be the last of it for the few months of winter. I guess it rained so much in this country that it was like an invitation for the weeds to sprout. To show the world and sundry that they existed—'Here we are! We're still here! Peekaboo!' I laughed to myself, as I slipped on the gardening gloves and dropped to my knees in my mother's front garden.

It was chilly too. I wished I'd brought my woolly hat, but my mother always commented that I looked like a homeless beggar in my knitted hat. I loved it, personally, and continued to wear it on the days when I was off duty with my mother, like going to work in the library. My colleague, Patricia, had knitted it for me with five different coloured balls of wool. I called it my rainbow hat and I loved it, even though it was getting a bit worn now. Maybe my mother was right. It was time to hand it over to the charity shop. I'd have a think about it.

I was almost finished pulling the weeds when it started to rain. The smallest ones were the most stubborn, but when I stood up to survey the driveway, I thought I'd done a pretty good job. I put the dirty gloves in my boot. I'd wash them and bring them back next time. I sneezed on my way in. I was dying for a hot cuppa, but my mother was resting on the armchair in the kitchen. I didn't want to disturb her by boiling the kettle, so I left her a note on the kitchen table. I tiptoed out, smiling to myself, knowing I could have the rest of the afternoon to myself. My weekend could finally begin!

Chapter Two

'God bless you,' Patricia, my colleague at the library, responded to my sneeze. 'Did you catch a cold over the weekend?' she asked.

'Em, yes, I think maybe I did,' I answered, thinking about how I didn't stop sneezing all evening after my driveway duties. I didn't even have the energy to steam my bathroom tiles in the end. I'd just curled up on the couch with some hot chicken soup, watching *The Big C*. I loved that show. I'd recorded all the episodes but fell behind since before Christmas. I had a lot to catch up on.

'Oooh, was it a late one? You must have been out with the girls. Did you meet anyone nice?' Patricia beamed. She wanted me to meet someone about as much as I wanted to meet someone.

'Oh, no, nothing like that. I was pulling weeds in my mother's driveway and got rained on,' I filled her in. Then a queue started to form so we didn't get to chat again until break time. One would never imagine it to be so, but there was a high volume of cattiness amongst librarians. Apathy mixed with bitterness filled my work environment. Patricia felt it too, so we always timed our breaks together to avoid spending an extra second with a toxic colleague. There was only a certain amount of negativity one could put up with on a Monday morning. Lately, the new guy, Ronnie, had started to join us too. He'd cottoned on to our escape plan and endeavoured to hop on board. We didn't mind. We let him in. He was harmless. And kind of funny too. The three of us enjoyed our breaks together.

'So, no fella then?' Patricia enquired with a cheeky grin. 'You hardly met someone pulling weeds in the driveway, hahaha!'

'No, all I got was a chill and a cold, unfortunately,' I admitted.

'What about you, Ronnie?' Patricia asked. 'Did you do anything exciting over the weekend?'

'I joined my local gym. I'm hoping to shed a few pounds,' he informed us as he tucked into his double chocolate chip muffin.

'Oh? You're on a fitness buzz, then?' Patricia looked interested.

'Yes, and it starts straight after this!' He gobbled down the last of his muffin and grinned. 'Ah no, seriously, I've two stone to lose.'

'Oooh, yikes, that's a lot,' I said, knowing that I could do with losing a few pounds myself. I carried it around my hips and tummy. I was pear shaped and as my mother always said, there was no hiding it at my height. If I was taller, maybe it wouldn't be so obvious, but I was only five foot three.

'It is,' he agreed, 'but I'm on a six-week program now at the gym, where I have to be accountable and check in with my fitness coach twice a week. There's a weigh-in and an assessment once a week and then I get tips and tweaks at the other check-in.'

'Oh? That sounds quite intense,' I said.

'It is, Emma, you're right. You see, I've tried and failed so many times to lose some weight and nothing has worked. I've been carrying this extra fat around since puberty if I'm honest. I'm thirty-seven now and I think it's hindering me from meeting someone. You know? I'm self-conscious about it.'

'Wow, I admire your honesty, Ronnie. Not a lot of people would admit to that,' Patricia acknowledged. She spoke my mind too.

'In fairness, before I started therapy, I wouldn't have admitted to it either. I've been seeing a therapist for a few months and he's encouraging me to be open and vulnerable. I was inclined to bottle up my feelings, you know, the shame I felt about my extra weight, but he said to be open about how I feel. So, if I'm trying to lose it, tell people. If I'm happy with my weight the way I am, then celebrate it. Sorry, am I sharing too much now? I'm at the early stages…'

'No, no, not at all, Ronnie,' I reassured him. 'It's refreshing to hear you speak from the heart. I mean, it's so common to bottle everything up and feel that shame. I think your therapist has a point.

It's good to talk,' I smiled. He nodded appreciatively and smiled back.

*   *   *

I got through the week with extra vitamins, that iron tonic my mother suggested and plenty of paracetamol to overcome the cold I'd acquired. Julia and Helen were going to a Thai restaurant and then a speed dating night. They invited me to join them. Speed dating didn't sit right with me at all. I'd love to meet someone organically, in an unforced way, but I guess that hasn't really worked out for me so far. I wore my new skirt and boots that I'd bought in Belfast and met them at the restaurant.

'Wow! You guys look amazing! Julia, you got a spray tan? I thought you said you were never getting that done again on account of the streaks last time?' I marvelled at their glamour.

'I know, I'm weak willed, though! There was a special on and I was seriously pale and run-down from work. I just needed a lift,' she informed me.

'Well, you look great! Like you're just back from the Bahamas!' I beamed.

'Oh, Emma, you're wearing your new clothes from Belfast! Very nice! Those boots sure do look comfy!' I could tell Helen was struggling to walk on the cobblestones in Dublin city centre in her kitten heels. I linked her arm when I saw how wobbly she was. It must have been a man who designed these pavements. No woman in her finery in Dublin could look elegant trying to get from A to B on these uneven surfaces. Maybe I'd look up Dublin street designers in the library on Monday.

'I knew you'd go for that! You're so predictable, Emma!' Helen laughed when I ordered the chicken and cashew stir fry.

'I know I like it and it's just the right amount of spice for me,' I defended my choice.

'Oh, Emma, you're so unadventurous when it comes to food,' Julia added. 'I hope you'll be more open-minded when it comes to choosing a man later, hahahaha!'

I joined in with the laughter, feeling a knot in the pit of my tummy. I was dreading the speed dating and didn't feel open-minded about it at all. And, I wasn't at all adventurous with my taste in men. I wasn't aiming for exoticism of any fashion. I just wanted someone nice. A decent, kind guy, that was relatively tolerable on the eye. That was all really. A companion, I suppose. I always thought it would be cosy to snuggle up on the couch with someone and share the news of my day. Of course, I had a biological clock too and it was ticking louder of late. So, I suppose there was a hurry of sorts. I thought I wanted to have a baby some day. The girls definitely did. They made no bones about it. It was on Julia's list of questions for her dates—'Do you want to have a family some day?' It was a deal breaker for her. Sometimes, I wished I had her confidence. I couldn't ever imagine asking a stranger that question.

We all agreed we'd have to meet the right guy first, though. I drank a couple of glasses of wine with my meal to get a buzz going. It worked. I felt a little more relaxed about the speed dating. Helen and Julia were super positive too. We all agreed on a meeting point afterwards to discuss potentials. Obviously, if one of us met someone that we wanted to go for a drink with after the session, then we would just chat the next day.

* * *

There were so many good looking people there. I felt old and very ordinary compared to the others. Our agreed meeting point afterwards was by the cloakroom where we paid two euros to hand in our coats, so we could parade around in our glamorous outfits. It was February in Dublin and I dressed accordingly, but when I surveyed the arena, I realised most people hoped February WAS actually the start of spring. There were short sleeves, tanned shoulders, goose-pimpled arms and long legs on show everywhere. I started to shiver.

The sight of bare skin in a cold February in Dublin made me uncomfortable.

We parted ways and went around the circuit of tables with bells on them. I knew I was in the wrong place with the wrong crowd when buzzers sounded as soon as I sat down opposite someone. Often, I didn't get a chance to say hello and had to move on straight away. It was cut throat. I couldn't wait for it to be over and I met no one I liked. Not one.

I waited for the girls at our designated meeting point. After fifteen minutes, when the queue died down, I went to retrieve my coat from the cloakroom. I wrapped up warm and cosy and waited another thirty minutes. No sign of the girls and no messages on my phone either. I guessed what had happened. They must have both met someone. My heart lifted when I realised the whole evening wasn't a total waste of time. The girls must have met someone they liked if they left the venue with them. I really hoped I'd hear good news from them. They both desperately wanted to meet the man of their dreams and tried so hard with excruciating nights like these. Oh, how I hoped it would work out for them. I rode home in the taxi alone, but with a hopeful smile on my face that Helen and Julia would have good news to report the next day.

They did. Those two. Both of them! It was unbelievable really. I never thought anyone would actually meet someone with potential at one of those contrived, speed dating nights. It seemed as though Julia's direct questioning had paid off and she met a guy that was as eager as her to get married and settle down. Helen met a guy called Mark who she agreed to go out with again. She wasn't sure about him, though. She mentioned he was a bit bland and might suit me better, but she was willing to give him another chance.

Hmmm, Mark, I thought, as I drove over to collect my mother. That sounded like a nice, dependable name.

'You're late,' she greeted me from her doorstep.

'I am? I thought mass started at twelve. It's only 11.30. We've plenty of time to get there,' I reassured her.

'I was hoping you'd finish what you started last week, before we go to church.' She gestured at the driveway.

'It looks okay to me, what are you talking about?' I couldn't see any weeds at all.

She came down the steps and pointed to a few gaps between the cobblestones.

'Look here,' she said, 'these need to be filled in with some sand. Sure, the weeds will pop out again in no time if those gaps aren't filled. You only half did it, Emma. It's a job half done.'

I felt my eyes water a little. I thought about telling her I'd been dying of a cold all week due to my efforts last weekend in her driveway. But we didn't have time for an exchange like that right now. Not if she wanted to make it to twelve mass. I wiped away the almost tears that I wouldn't allow to come and retreated to my car, where I took out the gardening gloves that I'd washed for her. I handed them to her and told her they were clean. She checked them, turned around and went to get her coat.

I took a deep breath and surveyed my mother's weedless driveway while I waited for her. I was thirty-eight years old. I needed my life to start soon. That thought that I constantly pushed away resurfaced again in my mind. I took another deep breath, deeper this time. The thought reappeared. It wouldn't go away. It was pleading with me to act on it. It was stubborn like the weeds. It had a voice. A niggling voice and it told me that a change was urgently required.

I needed to alter something in my life for it to move forward. Then, my mother returned with her handbag and umbrella.

'Don't just stand there,' she urged. 'I don't want to be late for mass.'

Chapter Three

Julia cast off Mark within a week. 'When you know, you know,' she always said, and she seemed to just know that Mark wasn't for her. She said she couldn't put her finger on it, but it seemed like a spark was missing between them. I encouraged her, saying that maybe she should give him a chance and a week really wasn't long enough to decide, but she'd already booked into another speed dating night the following weekend with her sister.

She did very charitably mention that she'd told Mark about me. As soon as she realised he wasn't for her, she let him know that she had a single friend. It was her way of letting him down gently. *Although you can't have me, I'm willing to pass you along to my less good-looking friend.* I'm sure she didn't mean for it to sound like that, but it kind of did. I didn't care too much anyway, because I doubted he'd ring. He'd probably go and book another speed dating night like Julia did.

At work, at breaktime, I shared the story of Mark with Patricia and Ronnie.

'Don't you dare take her seconds!' Patricia insisted. 'You're better than that. She shouldn't have given him your number without you even meeting him. That's not something a friend should do!'

'Oh no, I can assure you, she had my best interests at heart. We're all really rooting for each other in that department. We really want to see each other settle down. The three of us are in our mid to late thirties, you know, and if we don't act now our chances of having babies decrease rapidly.'

'But that's not right, Emma. Don't rush into a relationship to get pregnant with someone. Wait until you meet someone you like and take it from there. If it's meant to be, it's meant to be. What do you think, Ronnie?'

Ronnie wiped the crumbs of his blueberry muffin to the side of his face. 'Hmm? Me? Yeah, what you said, Patricia. What's for you won't pass you.' He took another bite and finished it off. We looked at each other and smiled.

'I like that,' I said. 'What's for you won't pass you.' Then we all said it together. A few times. Just because we liked it and we did silly stuff like that sometimes, as a threesome.

*   *   *

I was right, Mark didn't ring. He texted! He said he got my number from a friend and asked if I'd like to meet for a drink. Oh, so they're friends now, Mark and Julia. That must be how they left it. I replied and asked if an afternoon coffee would be okay instead. He joked about it, saying it might be easier for me to do a runner in daylight.

I liked him well enough so far. He'd made me laugh already and didn't waste any time executing our coffee date. He must have trusted Julia that I was a good catch and in turn, I trusted her taste in men. If he was good-looking enough to impress her during a speed date, then he was definitely good-looking enough for me. She tended to be hard to please.

I was looking forward to our date. It had been a while since I'd been on one and even longer since I'd had any success on one. I didn't know, but I had relatively high hopes for this one. I suppose he'd been picked for me. Matched to me, so to speak. I put Patricia's words out of my head and tried to stay positive. She meant well. She always did.

I met him in *The Coffee Society* in the city centre. I wore jeans, a bright cardigan and my long, light blue coat with a navy scarf. I thought I looked well. I was delighted Alan texted and told me he'd be visiting our mother today with Sophie. That got me off the hook and I could look forward to a guilt-free afternoon knowing that I wasn't letting my mother down by abandoning her. Alan would pull his weight today.

I arrived at the coffee shop embarrassingly early. I didn't think the bus would fly in like that on a Saturday afternoon. I guess there were no GAA matches scheduled, so traffic was considerably lighter. I was unsure whether to sit in and wait for him, maybe order my coffee and sip it elegantly until he arrived. I always thought there was an air of sophistication about people who sat alone in coffee shops, confidently, as if they didn't care if anyone joined them or not. They were just there for the coffee. Could I pretend to be one of them?

Nah, probably not. I'd just look frightfully insecure and be afraid to sip too much in case I finished it before my date arrived. Then if I was forced to order a second, I was fully sure the amount of caffeine in two lattes would send me off my rocker, so I thought it safer to pace up and down the street outside, channelling nonchalance.

'Emma?' I heard a voice behind me. When I turned around I was met with a tall, dark-haired, promising-looking man.

'Mark?' I asked. He smiled, nodded and offered his hand to mine. I shook it and smiled back. Yay, I thought, he's tall with a warm smile. This was a good start.

We went into *The Coffee Society* and he asked me what I'd like. He paid for my latte and bought a little pack of shortbread to share, even though I didn't order it. *Yay! Nibbles!* I delighted in the thought that he was a fan of nibbles too. We sat down by the window. The exact table I would have wanted, overlooking Liffey Street and the Saturday shoppers in town.

'Thanks, Emma, for agreeing to meet me. You know, under these circumstances. It was very generous of you.'

'Oh no, well, thanks for texting me, Mark. You made it happen.' We looked at each other and smiled. He had kind, bluey-grey eyes and a caring face. I noticed his manly crows feet and reckoned he was a little older than me. Mature—I liked it. I liked him. *Thank you, Julia!*

'So, speed dating wasn't for you? Julia said you went home early. Is that right?'

'Well, not exactly. I stayed the course, but didn't meet anyone, unfortunately.'

'Yeah, it's a shame our paths didn't cross. I wouldn't have hit the bell for you,' he smiled, showing me those glorious ripples around his smiling eyes.

'Oh, thank you, that's nice. Thank you for saying that, Mark.' We both sipped our lattes.

'So, did you have far to come today?' I asked, wondering where he was from, although his accent told me he was a Dublin man.

'Cabra,' he said. 'I got the bus. What about you?'

'Castleknock,' I smiled. 'I have an apartment. I bought it there a few years ago because it's close to my mother, where I'm from. I can be at her house in fifteen minutes. It's very handy.'

'Oh, how nice it is to be close to your mother. I can tell already that you're a good person. If you're a good daughter, you're a good egg.' We laughed. I liked that he liked that I was a good daughter. I was a good daughter. I just wished my mother thought so too.

We chatted some more about work. He was a banker with an interesting role in credit institution supervision in the Central Bank, not far from where we were having our coffees. I told him all about the library and he genuinely seemed fascinated. Neither of us fancied any more caffeine, so we took a stroll around the city. My heart filled with glee when he stopped to pet a dog. HE STOPPED TO PET A DOG! A sure sign that he was one to hold on to. Definitely had potential and he invited me to dinner the following Thursday night.

We sort of squeezed hands at the bus stop saying goodbye and I skipped on to the bus. I texted Julia straight away.

Emma
Just had a coffee date with Mark. He's fab, Julia! Thank you so much. We're meeting for dinner this Thursday! Xx

Julia

No problem! He's all yours. I thought you two might get along!

Emma
So far so good!

Julia
I'm going again tonight. Wish me luck! I'm hoping to meet someone far more exciting than Mark!

I paused before replying. Hmmm. Sometimes she could be a bit scathing. I was sure she didn't mean it though, or even realise it. I replied.

Emma
Good luck

But I didn't add any exclamation marks.

*   *   *

I couldn't wait to tell Patricia and Ronnie all about Mark, but to my dismay, Patricia had called in sick. I hoped I hadn't passed on my cold to her from last week. I wanted to text her to find out, but I didn't get a minute. Myself and Ronnie were run off our feet. Some days were just crazy like that and this was one of them. I could hear Ronnie panting every time he walked by. Poor thing, I thought, he really does need to shed a few pounds.

Patricia was the kids' activities co-ordinator in the library and when a class from the local school came to visit, we were lost without her. They wished to do research for their sixth class project on climate change. Patricia was due to receive them, show them the relevant section and go through some of the material with them. Ronnie asked me if I'd do it, but I told him I wouldn't have the confidence to address a group of thirty twelve-year-olds. I didn't think I'd be able to relate to them. Sure, they were almost teenagers! And, like, how does one communicate with teenagers these days? I wouldn't have a notion.

We asked around some of our other colleagues, but they mostly just laughed in our panic-stricken faces or rolled their eyes, saying, 'That Patricia—why does she bother organising all this stuff for the kids? Half the time the groups don't even show up.' In fairness they had a point. Patricia was stood up on many occasions by class groupings who promised to arrive at a certain time, but either didn't come at all or showed up at exactly the time she was due to have a break. And she always made such a huge effort. If it was a craft morning, she'd stay up half the night preparing for it. Or for a teddy bear's picnic with the toddlers, she'd bring in all her teddies from home and bake little cupcakes to share with the kids, the mammies and the teddies. For the Friday morning storytime with the preschoolers, she'd spend hours choosing just the right stories to link in with the theme of the month. When I thought about all she did for the local kids in the community, I realised SHE was the best resource this library had to offer.

Oh goodness, how we missed her that day. Fair play to Ronnie, he stepped up to take on the school group. No one else would do it and the teacher looked as though she might burst into tears after dragging a crowd of prepubescent kids to the library for a project they weren't showing much interest in. Most of them seemed to be drawn to the toddler section and all I heard was, 'Ah remember that? Did you like that one? *The Very Hungry Caterpillar*. Oh look, *The Tiger Who Came To Tea*', etc. They would have been happier to sit on the cushions on the floor and reminisce on their childhood favourites. If Patricia were here, she may have let them too. She always liked to see the kids having fun at the library. Otherwise, she insisted, they wouldn't want to come back.

Ronnie didn't give in to them like that, but rather directed them to the climate change section. I thought it would be a disaster and he'd lose them within the first few minutes, but he didn't start talking to them at all about the resources we had in the library. Instead, he asked them, 'So guys, tell me what you need? What exactly do you want to find out about for your project?' The teacher ensured they didn't all speak at once. She took a group or two with her and small groups came to Ronnie to request materials. It was a bit busy and noisy. He looked my way a few times and asked me to find certain books for them. I found everything they wanted and passed it to him. He remembered who had asked for what and in an hour they had all gone back to school with books to help them complete their project. I was amazed it wasn't a complete fiasco. They seemed happy with their productive visit to the library and the teacher gave us a big smile and a wave on her way out. I looked at Ronnie.

'We did it!' he exclaimed. 'They all got what they wanted! I can't wait to tell Patricia!'

I high fived him. 'That was all you, Ronnie. Well done! You were amazing with the kids! I couldn't have done it, honestly. I'm so impressed!'

He blushed. I laughed. Then, he laughed because he knew he was blushing and he knew I was laughing at his rosy cheeks. We had a right giggle about it and texted Patricia.

Chapter Four

Mark took me to an Italian restaurant on our date. I ordered the creamy chicken and mushroom pasta and he had pizza. He also ordered a bottle of wine and I found myself getting tipsy after the second glass.

He wore a blue check shirt and jeans with brown shoes. He looked good, although I could imagine how Julia wouldn't approve of his attire. Maybe he'd worn such clothes on their second date, but this would be far too casual for her. She liked a man to dress up and would expect a suit or at least smart-casual attire. It was certainly good enough for me, though. I thought he looked great and the blue shirt brought out the blue of his eyes. He admired my purple, floral top and I think we were both thinking the same thing when he stared into my eyes. We'd make a damn fine couple—that's what I was thinking, anyway.

Then, when he asked to see me again on Saturday, I realised we must be on the same page. We met in *The Coffee Society* again, then decided to catch a movie before dinner, which he'd booked in the same Italian restaurant. He was doing everything right and ticking all the boxes. The movie was sort of a 'well, will we?' kind of thing to pass the time, instead of browsing in the shops or going for a walk in the rain. We ended up deciding to see the latest Colin Farrell movie, even though we had no idea what it was about. Mark liked the cinema and had seen many of the other options. This one had just been released so we thought we'd try it. OMG, were we in for a shock! *The Killing of a Sacred Deer* was a mix between a very dark, black comedy and a horror. Not an ideal date movie, to say the least. I couldn't help bursting into laughter at the most inappropriate times and that set Mark off too. No one else seemed to be laughing though, which made it much harder for us to stop.

When we left the cinema we were in convulsions discussing what we'd just witnessed on the screen. It was so bizarre that it fuelled our conversation throughout dinner. It thrilled us that the movie seemed to have the same effect on both of us. It elicited similar reactions and that kind of thing was very important to me. If something so crazy like that movie had us sharing our perspectives like this, then I thought the more mundane things in life would be a breeze from here on. We were connecting and communicating and it all just felt so right.

We went for a drink after the restaurant. It seemed like neither of us wanted the night to end. Then he kissed me at the bus stop. It was a bit awkward at first when he leaned in and I didn't move, but he reached up and touched my chin and guided me towards his lips. We kissed and then we smiled and looked at each other and did it again. 'You're very special, Emma,' he said. 'I'm really glad I met you.'

I was walking on air at this stage and for the following days. *He likes me. He really likes me and I like him.* It felt wonderful. I felt attractive and worthy. I started fussing over my appearance because I wanted to look good. I wanted to look better. I started wearing makeup to work, because Mark said he might pop over to see me in the library someday if he could wrangle a half day. Patricia noticed. Of course, she noticed.

After a very successful toddler storytime when only two library books got torn, she called me over. Usually, I didn't walk through the children's section at toddler mornings, because the little ones tended to run riot and I wouldn't know what to do or say if one of them approached me. I liked to smile over at them though, from a distance. But on this day I heard Patricia calling me so I went over.

'Look at you, Emma! You look gorgeous! I love that pink lipstick on you. Is Mark picking you up after work?'

'Oh, thanks! Well, he said he'd try to pop over some afternoon to see me. He's only ever seen me with my makeup on, so you know, I thought I'd try to maintain the illusion!' We both laughed. Just then, a little boy came over and hopped on Patricia's lap. 'Hey Max! What's up? Look, here's Emma. Are you going to say hi?'

'Oh, I'd better get back to it. I'll see you later at break,' I tried to leave, but Patricia wanted me to stay. 'Max, say hi to Emma. Look, will we wave?'

I looked down at little Max. He copied Patricia and waved. He waited for my reaction, so I waved back. 'Now, will we sing our song for Emma?' Patricia bounced him on her lap.

'Ah no, you're okay. I've got loads of returns to deal with and…' They ignored me and started.

'Sing a song of sixpence, a pocket full of…' I stood there nodding and smiling, because I didn't know the words to join in. He was dead cute, though. Max had pudgy cheeks and long eyelashes. He was a stunning-looking child with an angelic voice. I was impressed he knew all the words and sang along with Patricia. I instinctively clapped when they were finished and he reached out to me for a high five. Myself and Patricia laughed. 'Ahhh,' we said in unison, as Max hopped down and ran to his mother. 'You can go now,' Patricia said. 'I just wanted you to meet Max.'

'He's gorgeous,' I replied, grateful that I'd met him. Later on during our break, Patricia asked me if I'd like to join her for the next toddler morning. Before I had a chance to say no, she reminded me of how cute Max was and how much fun it was to listen to his sweet singing voice. I tried to protest and let her know that I'd no experience with children, but she was having none of it.

'Here's your chance then, to gain some experience with kids. I won't hurl you into it or anything. Just shadow me and join in with some of the clapping rhymes. I think you'd be great, Emma, and you might surprise yourself.'

I really didn't want to, but it occurred to me that maybe the toddler mornings were getting too popular for Patricia to handle on her own. Perhaps she needed an assistant to help her out, being a victim of her own success. She'd been looking a bit tired lately and I could see why she'd choose me over the other librarians. We had a great rapport and always worked well as a team. I didn't want to see her struggling. She'd been such a supportive mentor to me over the years since I joined the library. I wouldn't ever want to let her down so I agreed to join in on Friday morning.

'What poems or stories will you be doing, Patricia? I should probably read over a few beforehand or the two-year-olds will know more than me!' I laughed and she joined in.

'Here,' she replied and handed me a treasury of children's nursery rhymes. 'A selection from this. I usually let the kids choose their favourite ones and we all sing along.'

Yikes, I thought. 'Great,' I said.

*   *   *

I went to the trouble of wearing makeup every day, but Mark didn't come. He texted me though and said he should be able to get away early on Friday. He told me it had been a crazy busy week at work. I loved that he worked hard. He was industrious. My mother would love that too. She'd be impressed with a banker. I hadn't mentioned him yet to her. I wanted to wait until we were more official. Of course, I shared every detail with Patricia and, as always, she was rooting for me. It was hard to get in touch with Julia and Helen as they'd both met someone of note lately. We missed each others' calls, but had shared a few texts about successful dates.

Friday was the morning I agreed to help Patricia out with the toddlers. She wanted me to check them in as they arrived. I was happy to do that as it only involved asking parents or childminders for contact details so we could keep them informed of relevant future events at the library. They were all so nice, friendly and appreciative of the library services for kids. Nearly every one of them mentioned how great Patricia was. I smiled and had to agree with each of them. That said, where the heck was she? Usually, she'd be here by now on the floor tickling some two-year-old, but there was no sign of her. It was getting close to the 10am start time. Ronnie must have clocked my anxious look and he came over.

'Ronnie, is Patricia in yet? They all seem ready to start.'

'I haven't seen her. I'll go and check the car park, two secs', and he was gone. Max crawled over and unzipped my boot. 'Oh, hi Max,' I said, glad that I remembered his name. How could I forget such an adorable child? Then, he zipped it back up again and I thanked him. He moved to the other leg and unzipped that one. Oh, it was a game now. I couldn't help laughing and was secretly glad this would pass the time until Patricia came. It looked as if I was engaging with the toddlers, because I was letting Max play with my zippy boots. And it was kind of fun. I kept catching his eye, exclaiming, *'oh'* with raised eyebrows, and then we'd both laugh before he zipped me up again.

Relief swept through me when I saw Patricia dashing over. Oh, I thought, she looks wrecked. I wondered if her grandkids had come for another sleepover. That always wore her out.

'Thanks for holding the fort, Emma.' She flew past me to her little book station. Max left me and followed her. In fact, they all did. They just seemed to gravitate towards her. She was like the Pied Piper commanding the children. They seemed to be naturally drawn to her, although I supposed they knew her at this stage due to their regular visits to the library.

'I'm glad you're here, Patricia. I was getting worried I'd have to handle this lot on my own,' I laughed.

'Don't be silly, you'd be grand if that was the case. You'd manage. I'm sorry, Emma, I had an appointment.' She looked flustered. I left her to it. I sat at the back and watched the sing-song and part of the story time. It was so much fun. I found myself clapping along once or twice. Then I got the evil eye from my colleague Hazel. She approached and announced that assistance was urgently required at the reception desk. What was she on about? I wondered. Friday mornings were always quiet, apart from the toddlers. I got up and made my way over just to check, only to be greeted by a wide-eyed, grinning Mark.

'Hey, I urgently require help in the psychology section to recover from a disturbing movie I saw recently. I haven't slept a wink since!' We both broke into laughter and he put his finger to my lip. 'Shush! We're in the library!' he whispered, very loudly, through his guffaws. I took an early break and swanned off with him to a coffee shop around the corner. Life was good! This had never happened before with any of my previous boyfriends!

Not that I had many to speak of...

Chapter Five

Things were moving fast with Mark. I told him all about the toddler mornings in the library and how Patricia wanted me to take a more proactive role in the children's section. He seemed impressed.

'I can see why she'd single you out for that,' he said, 'I'd say you're great with kids!' I gulped, not really expecting him to make comments like that so early in our relationship. We hadn't even slept together yet and he was laying loaded compliments like that upon me. At my age, this was a sensitive topic. While my friends, Helen and Julia, were gung ho on meeting a suitable father for their non-existent babies, I really hadn't fully committed to the idea of having kids yet. I guessed from Mark's enthusiasm that he had.

He clocked my reaction. 'Have you thought about having kids, Emma? Is that something you want?' I looked at him, willing the ground to swallow me up. I didn't know how to reply. He sensed my anxious uncertainty and laid his cards bare. 'Because I have. I've thought about it a lot. A heck of a lot, actually. And you'll probably guess, I'm all for it. I can't wait to be a dad someday. I'm forty and ready. I don't want to wait until I'm old enough to be a grandad!' He smiled when he said that, but I got the impression there was more to it.

'Have you ever been close to having a baby or meeting someone you wanted a family with, Mark?'

He looked down. 'I was wondering how long it would be until this came up,' he kind of laughed sadly to himself, before making eye contact with me again. 'I was with someone, Ger, for nearly ten years and we got engaged. She was kind of an impatient person and she wanted to test me out for fatherhood, I think, before we committed and got married. So, we tried for a baby and nothing happened, not for a long time. We didn't know why. She blamed me of course, wondering if all my cycling was contributing to my stunted sperm count, so I gave up cycling. We "postponed" the wedding and we got some tests done. She started taking hormones, oh, what's it called? Something beginning with c...'

'I wouldn't have a clue,' I offered, so he continued.

'Clomid, yeah, I think that's it. Anyway, whatever it was, it did the trick and she got pregnant.'

'Oh, so you've got kids? I didn't realise, you never mentioned,' I realised I sounded panicky.

'She miscarried that one and the next one and the third too. We stopped trying then, to give ourselves a rest. We both knew we had a rake of tests to undergo, but we were shattered and broken and neither of us could muster up the energy for the next step in the fertility process. The wedding plans fell to the wayside. We decided we should put all of our money into this instead and the wedding could wait. But, to be honest, all that disappointment we endured took its toll on our relationship and we didn't make it. We broke up three years ago and I heard she's with someone else now. No kids, so I think maybe it was her all along. I don't mean that to seem like I'm blaming her or anything. I'm sad for her, because I know how much she wanted a baby. But, I did too and it's not too late for me. I've just been waiting to meet someone. They never found anything wrong in my sperm tests or anything...' Then, he looked up and saw how uncomfortable I was. I may have looked terrified because I was.

'Oh, I'm sorry, Emma. This is way too much too soon, isn't it? I apologise, really I'm sorry, I just get carried away sometimes and my therapist encourages me to share.'

'You're going to therapy?' I asked, realising I didn't really know this guy at all. This guy that I was falling for.

'Yes, I find it helpful. I hope you don't mind my honesty.' He looked vulnerable, so I stepped closer and gave him a hug. He grabbed me tight and held me close. Wow, I thought, he really needs someone and he's sharing everything with me. I felt so wanted that I matched his intensity with my grip on him. This was the closest I could ever remember being with someone and it felt deeply profound and special. I liked that he opened up to me, trusted me and wanted me. We looked at each other and kissed. The following weekend, he stayed over in my apartment and we had sex. At the last minute, I asked if he had a condom, but he didn't. I slid out from under him and got one from my drawer. It may have been well out of date, but I figured it was better than nothing.

'Really?' he asked, when I handed it to him.

'I'm not ready,' I said and he put it on. When he entered me, I smiled and said, 'Yet.' His face lit up when he understood that I meant I wasn't ready yet. It gave him hope that I would be soon. In fairness, it was early days in our relationship.

*   *   *

I assumed Helen and Julia would be happier for me when I shared with them how fast things were moving with Mark. They were very measured in their excitement. Both of their prospectives had been dumped or deemed inadequate marriage material. When I told Patricia, she said maybe they were just jealous that my relationship was going so well. I thought about it and concluded that she was probably right. I didn't want to hold it against the girls though, because I knew how desperate they were to meet Mr Right.

Ronnie was still working out and we were starting to see the benefits of his fitness regime that was costing him a small fortune. I noticed he wasn't going for the muffins or eclairs with his coffee anymore, and ordering salads instead of baguettes. He seemed to be taking it seriously and looked chuffed when myself and Patricia commented.

'I feel better too, you know, emotionally lighter, as well as physically. The knock-on effect is amazing. My fitness program is coming to an end next week, but I really believe I'm going to carry on.'

'More power to you, Ronnie,' I cheered and we gave him a clap. He flexed his brand new biceps and we all laughed.

'You should carry on, Ronnie. Your health is your wealth,' Patricia added. She looked down after she said that.

'Is everything okay, Patricia?' I asked, realising I'd been so distracted by Mark's visit last Friday that I'd never enquired about her early morning appointment that rendered her late.

'Well, I wasn't going to say anything. I hoped I wouldn't have to, but I got some bad news, I'm afraid.'

Ronnie looked concerned. It was obvious he liked her as much as I did. 'What is it, Patso?' That was his pet name for her.

She put her head in her hands. I rushed to her side. This was not typical Patricia behaviour at all. When she spoke it felt like a punch in my tummy.

'It's cancer,' she said. 'I've got cancer and it's fairly progressive.'

'Oh God, Patricia.' I put my arm around her. 'Oh no, I'm so sorry.' We hugged. Ronnie came over and took her hand. He stroked it and said, 'Ah, Patso, how long have you known?'

She wiped her eyes and I gave her a tissue for her nose. 'Ah, look guys, it doesn't matter. I've known for a while, but didn't want to say anything until I got the all clear. But'—she sniffed—'the all clear I was hoping for never came. It's bad news, I'm afraid. It's terminal. They told me last week.'

'Oh my God, Patricia, how have you kept this to yourself?' I asked. More pertinently, Ronnie asked, 'And what the hell are you doing at work? Here, in the library? With cancer? Go home, Patricia. What are you doing here?'

'Ah Ronnie, that's what they're all saying to me at home too, but sure I'm down to part-time hours at this stage, only short half days, so I can organise events for the tots. What would I be doing with myself at home only driving me and everyone else mad with worry. The kids here are a great distraction and I look forward to our giggles at lunch hour before I go home. This is like a tonic for me. I'm not quitting until I have to.'

I hugged her again. 'That's the spirit, Patricia, that's the fighting spirit.'

That evening while driving home, I realised Patricia had ulterior motives with getting me involved in those toddler mornings. God love her, the poor thing, she wouldn't want to see the empire she'd built up in that library going to waste. Someone would have to carry on the kids' activities. All of Patricia's hard work would not be in vain. I vowed to dig deep and find it within me to make a success of it. I rang her the minute I got home.

'Patricia, what's the theme for this week? I'll source the stories and you tell me what nursery rhymes you were planning to do.' I urgently required my inner Mary Poppins to present herself and guide me now in my hour of need. I've always said it, I'd do anything for Patricia.

Chapter Six

Mark showed himself to be very compassionate when I told him the story of Patricia's illness. He asked if there was anything he could do. I thought about it and realised I wanted him to meet her. She was such a special person that I knew I'd be talking non-stop about her, so it would be good if he could put a face to her name. I also wanted to know what she would make of him. I imagined they'd get on. Mark was fairly easy-going.

On a different note, I shared the sad news of Patricia's diagnosis with my mother.

'Sure, she's as old as me. How old is she? And with grandkids too, sure what's she doing still working anyway? She should be retired. Working full-time at her age would give anyone cancer.'

'She's only part-time and she's a good ten years younger than you. She does short days and she works because she loves her job at the library. She loves being the kids' activities co-ordinator and…'

'Sure, that's just a glorified childminder.'

'Mother! No, it isn't. She's showing the children from a young age how much fun it is to visit their local library and fostering in them a lifelong love of books. I've seen it with my own eyes. Those kids from the toddler mornings continue to come back, because their local library is like a second home to them.'

She looked at me with surprise in her eyes. Maybe she'd never seen me so passionate about something. Then, she broke eye contact and mumbled.

'She's fond of the money, that one. Fond of the income. She does it for the money. That's the only reason why someone goes into work every day in their sixties.'

I exhaled deeply. I was exasperated, but I let it go. She just didn't get it. She didn't understand the brilliance of Patricia and I realised I had no hope of convincing her to look at it from my point of view. I had mentioned Mark once or twice in recent weeks. She changed the subject.

'I need hoover bags. Alan got the wrong ones.'

'Well, can't he bring them back and get the right ones?' I asked.

'He's away with Sophie until Wednesday and I need them urgently.'

'Urgently?' I was dubious hoover bags were urgently required.

'Yes. For Monday, when Lynn comes to do the cleaning. I need them by then.'

I had set her up with Lynn. When her foot became sore and her legs a bit shaky, I organised a cleaner to come once a week to help maintain the house. Of course, I used to do most of it, but her list of demands became too much for me, so I went and found Lynn. My saviour, I called her. I paid her 20 euros a week to do the cleaning. Mother said she couldn't afford a cleaner what with being a pensioner, although I was well aware of the thousands she had clocking up in her bank account, because I handled a lot of her banking requirements too. For paying bills and that kind of thing, I set up direct debits. Tedious, time-consuming work, but it was worth it when it was done.

'Well, I was going to take off now, because Mark is coming over and...'

'Oh, how convenient! The minute I ask you to do something, Mark is coming over.'

'Well, he is. It's not like I'm making it up or anything,' I remained calm and measured. It was the only way. I'd learned. The hard way, of course.

'And you're putting him first, are you? A man you met five minutes ago! You're putting him before me, are you?'

What's gotten into her? I thought about what Patricia said about my friends being jealous. Now, I wondered if my mother was jealous that I'd met someone. It didn't bear thinking about, really. It would actually depress me if I went there, so I took my car keys from the kitchen table and quietly told her I was going to get the hoover bags and I'd be back in half an hour. She called after me when I reached the front door to leave.

'Don't forget to return the wrong ones. They're under the chair in the hall. The receipt is in the bag.'

*   *   *

The traffic was busy on a Saturday afternoon and there was a long line in *Power City*. I texted Mark.

Emma

Hi, can you give me an extra hour? My mother needs help with something x

Mark

Was just about to leave... Good timing! Sure, no prob xx

I smiled to myself. He was great. I liked him so much and couldn't believe I finally had a real boyfriend. I still felt a sense of shock about the whole thing, especially when I thought about Helen and Julia still booking into weekly speed dating events. From their texts, I could see they were seeing the same faces each week and it was wearing them down. It was hard for me to know what to text back. I wanted to be sympathetic, but when I read over the texts I had typed, I was worried there was an air of smugness about them. They both knew how well things were going with Mark. I just didn't want to rub their faces in it, I suppose. They stopped asking me about him anyway. They didn't seem to want to share in my joy.

When I returned with the hoover bags, my mother asked, 'When will I meet him?'

'Pardon?' I was taken aback.

'Alan has introduced me to Sophie. When were you planning to introduce Mark to your mother?'

'Oh, of course, I suppose it's early days and…'

'Are you ashamed of me or something?'

'Oh no, of course not. Don't be silly! I'll have a chat with him later and…'

'He could come to mass with us tomorrow.'

Oooh, I'd been hoping to get out of that. I wanted to have a lazy Sunday morning breakfast with Mark instead, but now it seemed I'd missed my opportunity.

'I don't know about that. I don't even know if he's…'

'Catholic?' she asked.

'Well, religious, I was going to say. We haven't actually discussed that yet.'

'Sophie's Catholic,' she informed me.

'Is she?' I didn't know what else to say. I hadn't even met Sophie yet. 'Em, how about I check when Mark is free to pop around for a cup of tea? And I'll see you at the usual time tomorrow morning, okay?' I backed out of the kitchen before she had time to formulate an answer. It worked. I heard nothing, so I shouted 'bye' and made my escape.

*   *   *

'You're going to mass?'

Mark was both horrified and surprised when I told him he'd have to leave by 11am.

'Yes, I've to collect my mother at 11.30. I'm sorry, I tried to get out of it, but it's… I suppose it's really important to her.'

Then he did something I wasn't expecting. He leaned in and kissed me on the forehead.

'You're a good daughter,' he said.

I was stuck for words. No one ever acknowledged that fact before, not in my presence, anyway. And it was true. I fulfilled all of my mother's demands without protest. And without thanks. I did what I could, when I could. He was right. I was a good daughter. A damn good daughter.

I smiled back. He kissed me again, this time on the lips.

'And so humble too,' he said. 'I think I might be falling for you, Emma Ward.' His words cemented our relationship and we became somewhat inseparable after that. He called over midweek and at the weekends, between, before and after my mother's requested errands. We rang and texted on the other days and fell into a comfortable, steady pattern. I felt secure in our relationship, which I honestly don't think I'd ever managed before. I always wondered if my boyfriends liked me enough or maybe fancied one of my friends more, or sometimes whether I liked them enough to carry on with the relationship. I'd kissed some frogs, but everything felt just right with Mark. So far so good.

* * *

The day came when it suited Mark to meet my mother. She said he could come over for afternoon tea, because Alan and Sophie had cancelled.

'Am I just sloppy seconds?' Mark joked when he heard. I felt nervous when I realised he was actually excited about meeting my mother. I tried to keep it casual, but he arrived to pick me up in his work suit. Oh no, I thought, he wants to make a good impression. I should have been proud of him making an effort like that, but my stomach was in knots all morning. I just never knew how my mother would react to people and situations. She had surprised me on many occasions in the past and in most cases, not in a good way. Mark sensed my unease.

'Don't worry, Emma. I'll try not to embarrass you. I'll be on my best behaviour, I promise!' he tried to lighten the mood. If only he knew it wasn't him I was fretting about. It was my mother.

It went well to start with and Mark admired her lovely driveway, clear of weeds. They had a chat about the disadvantages of cobblelock drives on our way into the kitchen. When we sat down, she began to interview him about his 'line of work' and whether he was ever married before. He didn't flinch and answered politely, without giving too many personal details away. I was relieved. She wouldn't have anything on him. There wasn't much she could criticise him about.

She'd made sandwiches, scones and a pot of tea. Mark complimented everything from the strength of the tea to the amount of sultanas in the homemade scones. Everything was just right according to him. He kept making me smile with his gentlemanly behaviour. Everything about him screamed husband material to me that day.

We brought along some cakes for afters and Mark had given my mother a bunch of flowers too. He didn't put a foot wrong all afternoon and I showed him exactly how grateful I was the minute we got him home. We had a long, lovemaking session on the couch and I didn't even insist on him going to get a condom. He told me he loved me and I returned his words. I would have actually liked more time to reciprocate his kind words, but he said it just as he was about to enter me. He looked at me expectantly, awaiting my reply, so I just said it. I knew I really, really liked him and he made me happy, so that probably accumulated to feelings of love. And if it wasn't exactly full-on love that I felt for him now, I truly believed those feelings would come. It was just a matter of time.

*　　*　　*

The next day my mother rang with her weekly list of requests. She never said anything about Mark. She didn't pass comment either way and it disappointed me. I would have liked to know what she thought of him, but I suppose I only wanted to hear positive feedback. But, to my dismay, she said nothing. She didn't even mention his visit at the weekend.

I realised she'd mentioned Sophie to me on and off when she visited with Alan, so I wondered if she'd spoken of Mark with Alan. I rang my brother. He confirmed that she did mention meeting Mark.

'She did? And did she like him?' I asked, with the pace of my heartbeat increasing.

'Eh, she didn't say,' he said after thinking about it for a few seconds.

'Oh, well, did she say anything about him at all?' I pleaded.

'Em,' Alan uttered, casually, 'let's see.' I waited while he thought about it, as my heart pounded, as if getting ready to jump through my chest.

'Oh, she mentioned he'd brought flowers and cakes.'

'And?' Nothing from Alan. 'Did she like them?' I asked.

'Well, lilies aren't her favourite, because, you know, they're so much work with removing the stamen to avoid pollen stains.'

'Oh, I see.' I supposed Mark didn't consider the potential pollen stains. He just bought the biggest bunch of flowers he could find. Then Alan continued.

'And the cakes were too creamy. Too messy to eat in a civilised fashion, she said.'

This time I didn't reply. Alan spoke.

'Sorry, Emma. I wasn't sure if I should tell you, but you seemed as though you wanted to know.

You know Mam. She can be a bit blunt sometimes. She probably doesn't mean it.'

I realised his hesitation when I initially questioned him was him actually trying to spare my feelings and not him being absent-minded at all. I appreciated that. We arranged to go out at the weekend and meet each other's new partners. We ended up having a nice chat, both of us acknowledging that we should talk more often. He was a good guy, even though he didn't pull his weight with our mother. That said, she didn't exert the same level of pressure on him. The perks of being born male, I concluded.

Chapter Seven

Patricia had another early appointment. She didn't have to ask me this time to help out with the toddlers. I stepped up. I enrolled everybody first off and confirmed contact details. Then I greeted the toddlers, asking their names. Most of them replied, 'teddy' or 'ball' or whatever they happened to be looking at in the book at the time. Some just drooled and smeared it on my hand, but I shook their hands nevertheless, telling them how pleased I was to meet them. It was 10.15 and still no sign of Patricia so I swallowed my nerves and decided to start. I used a CD with background music to help me. My idea was to drown out my voice as much as possible. We sang 'The Wheels on the Bus' and 'Five Little Ducks'. They were brilliant and knew all the actions. I was grateful that mums and childminders joined in too. I caught Ronnie's eye and he gave me an enthusiastic thumbs up. It was going well so far, but I'd heard things could change from minute to minute in Toddler World. I wish I'd known I was about to experience that.

I turned off the CD and we tried to settle everyone on the mat for storytime. I was going to do a beautiful story that Patricia recommended to me, called 'Ruby Flew Too.' I fell in love with it when I read it during my prep. It actually brought a tear to my eye. When I told Mark, he kissed me and told me I'd make a brilliant mother some day. His comment made me squirm a little. I didn't know why.

Anyway, I suppose I just wasn't as engaging as Patricia or as child friendly or something, because I lost them after the first two pages. And, when I say I lost them, I mean I LOST them. Two of them started pretending they were ducks and waddled off. When the moms realised they were wandering out of the kids' section, they left their younger siblings to go and retrieve them. Then, the younger siblings had freedom to crawl around and they did. There was biting, fighting, spitting and rolling. A one-year-old that I was meant to be keeping an eye on rolled away from me at lightning speed. I had to crawl over in my skirt and boots to grab her. All of a sudden, I was on the floor with this baby on my lap, frantically looking for her mother to come back.

The two moms were gone a while, so I realised the toddlers must have gotten quite far into the adult section. I just hoped they didn't escape from the library altogether. This kind of chaos never occurred when Patricia was in charge. Other parents jumped in to retrieve the spitting culprits and when I looked up, I saw Patricia approaching with a toddler in her arms. Ronnie was behind her and I do believe I noticed him burst into laughter as I wrestled with this demon baby between my legs.

Patricia reached the storytime mat, where we were all rolling around biting each other. She immediately launched into 'If you're happy in your nappy, clap your hands', and to my relief, at least fifty percent of them stood up and joined in. The other escapee returned with his mortified mother and she took the rolling lunatic from me. Ronnie offered his hand to help me up off the floor and broke into more fits of laughter.

'Remind me to have emergency services present for your next toddler morning, Emma,' he said. That set me off and we had to run and hide in the adult section while Patricia distracted the attendees with her super powers. I looked on in awe after I recovered from my outburst. Myself and Ronnie observed how captivating Patricia was with the infants. We both understood why she came to work every day, even though she was dying. We could see it was her calling. Those kids got her out of bed in the morning. They excited her, thrilled her and wore her out, but in a good way. I felt like we were the only two librarians who appreciated Patricia. We looked at each other and choked up at the thought that she would be leaving us soon.

I don't know who reached for who first but we hugged, attempting to support each other in our premature grief. I was so glad I'd still have Ronnie and was certain he felt the same about me. We stood and hugged right there in the middle of the adult romance section, not even caring who was looking at us. All of the staff were aware now of Patricia's prognosis, so they must have guessed the source of our teary-eyed hug. I don't think either of us gave a hang what they thought, though. We just enjoyed the consolation we offered each other, based on our mutual love of Patricia.

*   *   *

Mark asked if he could take me away for the weekend. He wanted us to go to County Wicklow, also known as 'The Garden of Ireland'.

'In springtime, Emma, it's amazing. You have to see it. The newly opened flowers in Mount Usher, the newborn animals in Glenroe Farm and a walk on the expansive Brittas Bay Beach, where we can collect shells to our hearts' content.'

My cheeks hurt a bit from smiling. 'It sounds idyllic, Mark! When were you thinking of?'

'Next weekend? The weekend after? What suits you?'

I sighed. The weekends were when my mother needed me most. She was okay Monday to Friday because she had her activities in the day care centre to go to, but seemed to be at a loose end every weekend and the jobs clocked up. I realised we were due to double date with Alan and Sophie on Thursday evening, so maybe I'd see if he could step in while I went away with Mark. I explained this to Mark.

'I'm surprised she expects so much from you, if I'm honest,' he admitted. 'She seemed very sprightly and capable when I met her, and she has a car in the garage, doesn't she? So she can still drive.'

'Yeah, she can, and maybe from Monday to Friday she does when I'm at work, but she leaves the longer journeys for the weekends when I'm available, you see.'

'But what if you're not available? What if you want to escape away for a dirty weekend in Wicklow with your boyfriend? What then?'

I laughed. 'We'll see what Alan says. He might be able to help out.'

'Yeah, you guys should probably be sharing the care of your mother more evenly anyway. Why do you seem to do the bulk of the chores?'

I shrugged. 'She doesn't seem to ask him. He's always got stuff on at the weekends. I guess I was normally freer, until I met you.' We caught eyes and smiled.

'I do eat into your time a lot, Miss Emma Ward, don't I? Please accept my heartfelt apologies.' He curtsied. I reached out to him and we kissed. 'I'll see if Alan can take over for the weekend, okay?

Don't worry, we'll definitely make it to Wicklow at some stage and do all those lovely things, I promise,' I reassured him.

* * *

We met with Alan and Sophie on Thursday night in the city centre in a swanky tapas bar. Sophie was beautiful with long, blonde hair and impossibly large green eyes. I could see immediately what my brother saw in her. I wondered why my mother never commented on her appearance. Her beauty was undeniably striking. All I knew from my mother was that she came from money, was Catholic and had a pointy nose. I looked again. She had a perfect nose, long and straight. I'd die for a nose like that.

Alan was charming as always and seemed to hit it off with Mark. Sophie was interested in my job in the library and indulged me when I proceeded to speak about it at length. Honestly, I could talk all night about the library because I truly believed it was the best place on earth, but I didn't want to bore the poor girl to tears so I enquired about her job too. She worked in a high-end fashion retail outlet but wanted to get into fashion design. She had recently signed up for a six-month course and let it slip that herself and Alan were moving to London.

'Oh? I knew nothing about this,' I was shocked. 'When are you planning to move?'

She looked as though she'd accidentally put her foot in it and thought it would be better if I spoke to Alan about it instead. She nudged him and let him know that I knew about their impending move. I waited for Alan to talk to me and while I did, Mark struck up a conversation with Sophie.

Alan was thinking about how he'd break the news to me. 'So?' I asked. 'What's this about you moving to London?'

'Yeah, about that, I'm sorry, I should have been the one to tell you. Sophie didn't know I hadn't gotten around to it yet.'

'And? What's the plan?' I was eager to find out more.

'Em, well, the week after next we're heading over. Sophie booked the flights last week.'

'What? Why so soon?' I asked.

'A space became available in the fashion course she wanted to do. She thought she'd have to wait until next year for it, but they had a cancellation and offered her a place. It's what she wants to do and…'

'Mmhmm, yes, she told me. What about your job? Can you just…?'

'They have offices in London too. It's easy enough to get a transfer.'

'Oh.' My shoulders dropped and I felt myself getting sad. 'And what about Mother? Does she know?'

Then his shoulders dropped too. 'No, not yet. I'll tell her tomorrow. I'll call over tomorrow night.'

'Good luck,' I offered and we laughed. It was always tricky to break news like this to our mother. She didn't take it well when it was clear we were moving on with our lives.

'Look, I know I'm dropping you in it now with Mum and she needs more and more help as she gets older, but it's only for six months and I'll make up for it when I come back, I promise.' I looked at him. He was a lovely brother, a great guy. I could see what Sophie saw in him. But, unfortunately, I didn't believe or trust him. He'd let me down on so many occasions when it came to looking after our mother. He just didn't seem to possess the same levels of guilt that I did when it came to her care. Lucky him, I thought, and he gets away with it. Probably because he was so nice and charming and affable. I kind of thought I was all of those things too, but I got away with nothing. I'd get pulled up and questioned about every little move. Each baby step I took had to be accounted for. It had always been like that. I couldn't remember it ever being any different.

I sighed deeply, thinking, here I am, left on my own, the only daughter. Then I looked towards Mark and thought about how much I wanted this weekend away with him. That niggling feeling came back—a change was urgently required.

Chapter Eight

We stayed out kind of late with Alan and Sophie so I thought I wouldn't have the energy for the toddlers on Friday morning. However, the minute I saw them being carted in by their parents and guardians, I surprised myself with my enthusiasm. I remembered most of their names and they remembered me. I got hugs and high fives as I went around with the obligatory enrolment sheet. Max made a beeline for my zippy boots and we played the same game all over again.

When Patricia arrived after her early morning appointment, she looked exhausted. She was starting to look like a sick person now and she knew it, but no one said anything to her because she knew that we knew that she knew it. So, what was the point? She was here to work and have some fun with the kids and I was going to support her in any way I saw fit.

Her voice was gravelly. The cancer had travelled to her throat and she found that she couldn't sing this morning. Crap, I thought, I can't sing to save my life. I ran for the CD player and backing tracks. Ronnie saw me scrambling for CDs and came to my rescue.

'Good news!' he beamed. 'I can sing!'

I gave him a hug, so relieved was I.

'Yeah,' he said. 'I always fancied myself as a Gary Barlow tribute and if it wasn't for the bit of extra weight, you'd see my name in lights.'

'Oh? And did you have a tribute act name?' I asked.

'I sure did,' he said, looking very pleased with himself, as he got set up for the gig.

'Well? Aren't you going to tell me?' I looked wide-eyed. He had this way of surprising me with revelations from time to time.

'Barry Garlow!' He nodded, waiting for my approval.

I burst into laughter, bending over, holding my tummy. One of the infants approached and asked if I needed to do a wee. 'Why, yes! Yes, I do indeed!' I said as I rushed off, still laughing.

When I returned from the bathroom, I was taken aback with what I saw and heard. Ronnie was standing in front of the group with a toy microphone, teaching them the words and actions to 'Morningtown Ride'. It was the sweetest thing I'd ever seen. Even Patricia, who was sitting on a stool with one of the little ones on her lap, had a tear in her eye as she sang along. As for me, I just stood there watching. I felt twitches in my tummy, like little rolls and tumbles, but in a good way. A soothing sensation overcame me and I just felt, I don't know, warmth or something?

He taught them the first verse and the chorus and they loved it. I watched him perform a miracle before my very eyes, as they sang and followed the actions, not taking their eyes off Ronnie. He had them captivated, mesmerised, just like Patricia did every Friday, but this was unexpected because it was his first time.

Then Patricia looked towards me with her teary eyes. We both nodded in awe. No words were exchanged but we knew what each other was thinking—'He's bloody amazing, isn't he?' was what I imagined it was.

When he finished, he sat them all down and told them Emma was going to read them a story about trains, called the 'The Train Ride'. He told them they were going to LOVE it and they smiled and clapped enthusiastically. I stepped forward and sat on the story chair and guess what? I read the story with passion because I knew I was reading it for Patricia. Because I knew I had to show her that her work had not been in vain. Because I knew it was up to me and Ronnie to carry on these toddler mornings and I had to prove to her that we could. We could because we'd learned from her. We'd absorbed her energy and commitment and we were going to drive her legacy forward.

Whatever the motivations were for my performance of the story, it worked. The children were engaged, both asking and answering questions.

They made sound effects and climbed up on my lap to get a closer view of the pictures. Then Ronnie set up a little toy train station behind them with enough squishy, noisy things to keep them all happy. The library had funding to supply toys and books to accompany each theme we covered and Patricia kept everything in neatly labelled boxes for future use. This meant that when the funding was inevitably withdrawn, which it was from time to time, we still had supplies to dip into and reuse. Ronnie must have gone into the store room and sourced this box.

Patricia put her hand over her mouth. 'Do you know,' she said, with a shaky voice, 'I totally forgot I had those! Ronnie, how long did it take you to dig them up?'

He laughed. 'I stayed after closing time yesterday evening, just to explore what was in there. I found some brilliant stuff, especially with summer coming up. And then I remembered the theme for this month was travel, so I knew the train set would come in handy.'

She looked at both of us. 'You two are amazing! What a team! You're going to make this the most popular children's library in the country! They'll be travelling down from Donegal to come to our toddler mornings!' We all laughed, proud that we'd pulled it off. Then, Max's little brother pooped on the beanbag, so we had to evacuate the children's section until it got cleaned up. A successful morning overall, though!

* * *

That night I rang Alan to see how it went, breaking the news to our mother about his impending move to the UK.

'Not so well,' he informed me. 'She blames Sophie entirely. But the good news is you're in her good books now. She said Emma would never abandon her like this.'

'Really? I'm hardly ever in her good books!' We both laughed, because it was true. I explained to him about Mark's intention to whisk me away to Wicklow for the weekend. I told him we couldn't go this weekend as we had nothing booked. Therefore, next weekend would be our only chance, so as not to leave Mother with no one calling at the weekend. I asked if he could stick around to help her out, to give me an opportunity to get away with Mark. My heart sank a little when he told me their flights were booked for Sunday morning, but he reassured me he'd pop over to her on Saturday and get whatever she needed done.

I really hoped that would satisfy her because the minute I told Mark, he had the hotel booked. He made reservations for two nights, so we both booked the Monday off work.

Julia rang me over the weekend, asking me how it was going with Mark. When I told her we were going away for the weekend, she sounded genuinely delighted for me. Of course, with that, she launched into the wonderful story about how she'd met the most amazing guy recently and it was getting serious. So serious in fact that she was considering moving to Cardiff with him as soon as his contract ended in Dublin.

I told her I was happy for her and I was. But I was also feeling a bit down. Everyone seemed to be leaving me. Alan was going to London, Julia to Cardiff and Helen had stopped ringing because I think she was feeling bitter that she hadn't coupled up with anyone and her friends had. But the one that hurt the most was Patricia. I didn't know how much time she had left, but I knew from looking at her, it wasn't long. I would miss her the most. And, unlike the others, she would not be coming back. I got choked up every time I thought about it.

Then, an image of my mother sprang to mind. God forgive me, but if it was her with the terminal diagnosis, it wouldn't hit me so hard. I didn't think I'd miss her as much as I was going to miss Patricia. I might even feel a sense of relief if… And then I stopped my thoughts from going there. That was the dark side and I wasn't that kind of person. Or if I was, I was hiding it pretty well. For now anyway.

＊　　＊　　＊

After I'd run around doing errands with my mother and for my mother, I dropped her home. Mark was calling over later and I wanted to get home and shower and cook something nice for us. I was hoping to drop and go, but Mother had other ideas.

I pulled into her driveway, expecting her to get out, but instead, she turned to me. 'I suppose you'll be up and leaving me too, now that you have Mark. Just like Alan is with Sophie.'

'What? No, no I'm doing nothing of the sort. And Alan is only moving to London to support Sophie while she goes to college for...'

'Alan mentioned you were going away.'

'Oh, yeah I am, but only for a long weekend. I'll be back on Monday.'

'Who's going to bring me to mass?' She looked forlorn.

'Alan will be here all day Saturday. Isn't there an evening vigil mass? He could take you to that.'

'It's Bernadette's husband's second anniversary mass on Sunday at 12. I told her I'd go and now I've no way of getting there.'

'Well, em, you do have a car in the garage. Maybe you could drive yourself?'

'You know I only drive that car locally. The special mass is held in the church on the MacMillan Road, where Bernadette lives. I wouldn't dream of driving out there alone.' She looked offended, as if I'd hurt her for mentioning that she had a car and was able to drive it.

'What about one of the neighbours?'

'You've gone very cold since you met Mark. You've changed, Emma,' she said accusingly. I didn't quite know how to respond, so I didn't. She continued.

'There was a time when you'd answer my call in my hour of need and help me out, but I hardly see you now that you've shacked up with…'

'We haven't shacked up. We don't live together. He just calls around at the weekends.'

'Well, why can't he call over during the week and then leave our little routine the way it was at the weekends?' she enquired innocently.

I took a deep inhale. And exhale. 'Because we both work full-time and the weekend is the only time off we have to relax and see each other.' She huffed at that. It was like she didn't believe me. I turned to her. 'Mother, aren't you happy that I've finally met someone? Someone that I actually like and likes me back. I'm thirty-eight years old and have been living alone all my life and now I have a chance with Mark. A chance to settle down with someone and…'

'And where will that leave me? Where? If you get married and Alan's in London, who's left for me? I'll decay in that house, left all alone, I will.' She pointed towards the house.

I got out and helped her out of the car. I brought her inside and boiled the kettle. I took some buns out of her tin and put them on the table with a cup of tea for her.

'I'll bring you to the anniversary mass next Sunday,' I said as I walked out the door and left her, on her throne, with tea and cakes…to decay.

Chapter Nine

Wicklow was everything that Mark had built it up to be. Of course, I'd been there many times, given it was our neighbouring county, but not to the specific locations that Mark took me to.

The flowers in the gardens of Mount Usher were breathtaking. We got to cuddle the baby animals at Glenroe Farm. We made sure to get there bright and early, before all the families with kids would be arriving. We saw what we wanted to see and left just as the queues began to form. We had Brittas Bay Beach scheduled for Sunday, but I hadn't told Mark that I'd have to make a quick trip back to Dublin before we left for the beach. We were having a lazy morning in the hotel when I mentioned it.

'What? You've to head back to Dublin? You're joking, right? Emma! We're on a weekend away. It'll spoil it for you if you go back today.'

'It won't, I promise. And I won't be long. She just needs a lift to the church and then I'll drop her home afterwards. I'll be back here by two o'clock. We can spend the whole afternoon at the beach. It's only a short drive from here, isn't it?'

'I know. I'm just in shock that you're only telling me now, that's all. Why did you leave it until the last minute?'

'I suppose I didn't want to think about leaving you until the time came,' I said.

'So, you don't want to go, do you?' he probed.

'No,' I said.

'Why go, then? You shouldn't be doing things you don't want to do.' He was staring intently at me and I felt a little uncomfortable. I ran my fingers through my short brown hair a few times.

'Yes, I know, but she's my mother and she needs me.'

'Do you think she might be taking advantage of your good nature, Emma? I don't mean to be harsh, but this is your one weekend away and she's asking you to cut it short.'

He was right. I knew it, but couldn't bring myself to admit it. 'I'll be back at two and we'll have a great day, I promise.' I went to get ready. The newspaper was in the room and the hotel grounds were beautiful, so I knew Mark wouldn't get bored.

* * *

As I drove to my mother's, I realised that Mark could have come with me. I didn't think to ask and he didn't think to offer. At least she was ready when I arrived to pick her up. That was a good start. I accompanied her into the church, as I wanted to see Bernadette. It was busy so we waited a while for her outside to have a chat, or as my mother put it, 'to let her know we were here'. Bernadette finally arrived and we hugged and squeezed each other. I noticed my mother just smiled, nodded and looked on, but didn't offer Bernadette any affection.

'Thank you both so much for coming. It means a lot to me, you're very good. How about coffee back at my place? You're more than welcome. I'm well stocked up, because some of the neighbours will be around later…'

'Oh, I'd love to but I have to get back to Wicklow. My boyfriend is waiting for me and…'

'Oh, my goodness, Emma! You get back to him right now and don't mind us old fogies! We'll do that coffee some other time.' She hugged me again and was called away by another friend.

I looked at my mother. 'So, let's get going, yeah?' We walked towards the car and the minute we got in, she began. 'How rude of you to fob Bernadette off like that! I'm ashamed and embarrassed you wouldn't even go back for one measly cup of coffee. We could have been polite and stayed for ten minutes. I don't know what's wrong with young people these days!' She looked away into the distance.

I realised I had a short journey ahead of me to get through in order to drop her home, so I refrained from engaging for fear I might crash the car. We drove in silence. I pulled into her driveway, thinking she might have calmed down and maybe she'd feel bad for what she said, but she turned away from me and let herself out. I didn't know why I'd always walked around to help her out of my car. She was perfectly capable. I stayed in the driver's seat, wondering if she'd have a change of heart, but no. She turned the key in the door and disappeared into her house without a backward glance.

I sat in my car and practised breathing. It was an effort to inhale and exhale. It was an effort to stop tears streaming down my face too. They came and landed on my blouse. I searched my handbag for tissues and wiped them away. I blew my nose and reversed out of the driveway. Damn, I thought, as the tears trickled down once again. It was hard to drive through watering eyes. I took my time and drove slowly.

* * *

I had to stop for petrol, so by the time I got back to the hotel, it was after three. Mark wasn't in the room. I wondered if he'd gone to the beach without me. When I texted him he said he was walking around the hotel grounds. I went to join him. The sun had gone in and I wished I'd brought my jacket.

'Well? How did it go?' he asked. I could tell he had the hump.

'It went,' I said. 'Mark, I'm sorry I'm a little later than I thought I would be. I had to stop for petrol and…'

He cut me off. 'It doesn't matter. I think we missed the best part of the day.'

I looked up at the overcast sky and had to agree with him.

'Can we still go? I'll wrap up and we'll just take a walk. What do you think?'

At that very moment my stomach rumbled. We laughed. 'Let's get you something to eat first. You didn't get lunch, did you?'

He put his arm around me, so I took that to mean he forgave me for abandoning him. I ordered a toasted sandwich and gobbled it down, before going to the breezy beach in Brittas Bay.

'It's beautiful here! I can't believe I never visited it before.'

'Yeah, it's one of the sandiest beaches in Ireland, I think.' We held hands and walked and stopped every so often to look at a shell or the horizon or the sky changing colour. We walked in silence for a little while too and I really couldn't remember ever feeling so happy and content. After the low feeling of disappointment with my mother earlier, this was the lift I needed. He was looking after me and fulfilling my every need at this time.

We made love when we got back to the hotel. I didn't insist on a condom and he didn't reach for one. I think we'd arrived at an understanding now—it seemed like we had found everything we were looking for in each other. I cried that evening after our lovemaking. When he asked me why, I looked at him and said, 'You make me so happy.' He kissed me on the forehead and we curled up together to watch a movie. We ordered room service for dinner and made the most of our last night in the hotel.

I was glad the upset from earlier didn't spoil our weekend.

* * *

On our drive home from Wicklow, Mark told me he'd like to see more of me. He said once midweek and half a weekend wasn't enough. I felt he was hinting at me getting a key cut for him so he could drop over any evening after work. I offered it to him, thinking that was what he wanted, and he gratefully accepted.

I shared the news with Patricia and she started humming, *'I'm getting married in the morning'*. I laughed and looked towards Ronnie for his reaction. He just smiled and said he was happy for me. Then he added, 'If you're happy, I'm happy.' I thought that was a nice thing to say and I thanked him. Then Patricia changed the subject and told us the sad news that next week would be her last week in work. She said she needed to rest up for a while. She was planning to come along on Friday to enjoy one more toddler morning with us, and then the following Wednesday would be her last day. I caught eyes with Ronnie and we both looked down at the same time.

Driving home that evening, I started fantasising about my mother having terminal cancer instead of Patricia. When I thought about how serious Patricia's illness was, I got so choked up, I had to pull over and take a breather. I would never tell anyone, but I secretly wished it was my mother's diagnosis. I could handle that news much easier than Patricia's. I'd be able to deal with it with much less, I don't know, emotion.

I'd be great too. I'd drive her to all her appointments and liaise with the doctors. I could be the ideal daughter, if I thought there was an end in sight. Who knew, maybe even my mother would tell me she was proud of me from her deathbed. It could happen, if that were our scenario. But it wasn't. I didn't share my private thoughts with Mark later on. Instead, I asked him if he wanted to accompany me on Sunday to attend to some errands for my mother. He said yes.

We rang the doorbell at 11.30. While we waited, I briefly told him we had words last weekend.

'Oh? You never said. Is everything okay now?' he asked.

'I don't know.' I shrugged. 'I haven't had any contact since.'

'Gosh! Sounds serious! You can tell me later,' he whispered, as a shadow loomed in the frosted glass doorway. She didn't smile nor grimace, but we got a neutral nod in our general direction. I noticed she was ready for the lift with her coat on and handbag in tow. She unlocked the porch and Mark offered her his hand to help her down the steps.

'How are you, Angela?' he enquired.

'Fine, thank you,' she answered, and we got into the car to drive to mass. Mark helped her out and accompanied us into the church. He squeezed my hand in boredom a few times and I looked at him and smiled. After mass, he asked my mother if she'd like to go and get some afternoon tea in a nearby tea shop. It opened every afternoon and served dainty sandwiches and scones, along with delicious pastries, presented in quaint, willow-patterned tea delf. It was the type of place aimed at retirees, such as my mother. She agreed to come along with us.

The conversation was stilted at first, but Mark pushed and eventually they got into a flow. I had minimal involvement, noticing that my mother wasn't looking my way or trying to include me. Already, she seemed to prefer Mark to me. Just like she'd always preferred my brother, Alan. She seemed to have exorbitantly high expectations for me, but not for Alan. I bore the pressure of those expectations for 38 years and I was getting tired of it. It was lovely to have Mark with us to defuse the tension. I was glad of his support. I realised there and then that he would play a pivotal role in my plan for change. The change I hoped was coming, was entering my mind with greater frequency of late. When I thought of it, it made my breath quicken. It was down to both nerves and excitement—this realisation that a new life direction was urgently required and, quite possibly, imminent.

Chapter Ten

Ronnie brought his ukelele in on Friday and had the toddlers dancing around the library like lunatics. It was so much fun. I stood by the exit of the children's section to ensure no one escaped with all the excitement. He was so amazing with them that I couldn't help clapping along. I was beginning to understand the cathartic effect Patricia got from these gatherings. Just watching the children jump around completely uninhibited was liberating and made me want to join in. The atmosphere was electric and I even noticed some of the other librarians peeping in to check out the fun.

I got the look from Ronnie and realised I was up. Between us, we settled them down onto the story mat and I sat on a low stool amongst them. I looked up to show them the front cover and spotted Patricia in the corner. I smiled and waved and she gave me a thumbs up, before gesturing for me to carry on. So I did. I read the story with expression that I channelled from my two years of speech and drama lessons as a teenager. My mother had thought there was something wrong with me because I was so timid in secondary school, so she sent me to speech and drama to get me 'fixed'. Whilst there, we discovered there was actually nothing amiss. I joined in with all the elements and even passed one or two exams. The speech and drama teacher explained to my mother that I just needed time to acclimatise and feel comfortable before coming out of my shell. My mother withdrew me from the lessons and told people I was just awkward in company and not to take any notice of me. I tried to tell my mother that I didn't feel awkward at all. I just preferred to get to know someone before opening up and being at ease with them. To this day, I remember her reaction. She raised her eyes and told me she wished I was more like my brother.

Anyway, the two years weren't wasted. I could read a children's story with clarity and vigour. We all threw our heads back in laughter every time the tiger gobbled something else up. We had a great time and when it was over, parents brought their little ones up to me to say thanks and wave bye bye. Yet again, I understood the buzz Patricia talked about. This was why she still came to work while battling terminal cancer. I comprehended the payoffs. And relished them.

I was dying for my morning cuppa, but Patricia always tidied up after the toddlers and left the place spotless so I felt compelled. The parents had chipped in and picked up the majority of the books so it didn't take too long. Ronnie approached and gave me the coffee break symbol, which was an ascending cup-shaped hand. I hurried the last few books as I didn't want to miss Patricia. She had said she'd only be in for short days.

I got to the coffee dock and found Ronnie waiting for me with two steaming cups and a small bag of croissants. My heart lifted. How did he know? How did he know that was just what I wanted?

'Ah, bliss! You're a star, Ronnie!' I beamed.

'Enjoy,' he answered, but he didn't match my enthusiasm. I guessed he was probably tired, as he'd been single-handedly covering most of Patricia's shifts while she was out sick. And then I also wondered if he was disappointed in himself for eating buttery croissants, considering he was meant to be watching his calorific intake in order to shed those few extra pounds. That said, he looked as though he'd lost a stone or two since he'd started his new regime a few months ago. He was looking great, but tired, or sad, or something. I decided to investigate.

'Are you okay, Ronnie? Tired?'

'Hmmm?' He looked up with a mouthful of flaky croissant. 'Oh, yeah, I'm okay. Well, just heartbroken, I suppose.'

Oh gosh, this was the first time I realised I talked incessantly about Mark, Patricia constantly mentioned her husband and neither of us ever thought to ask whether Ronnie was in a relationship. We didn't even know if he had a girlfriend. I felt so selfish at that particular moment, especially because Ronnie was such a good listener and always displayed gestures of goodwill when I disclosed how it was going with Mark.

'Heartbroken? Ronnie, did you break up with your girlfriend? I'm so sorry I've been so selfish and never even asked if you…'

'Emma!' He looked at me with some sort of caution in his green eyes.

'What?' I asked with innocence in my hazel eyes.

'It's Patricia,' he answered, looking down. He left the rest of his croissant on the table then. I knew he wasn't planning to finish it.

'Where is she? Is she joining us for coffee?' I perked up and looked around.

'Emma,' he said again, 'it's very serious now. She…she couldn't walk today. Her husband pushed her in a wheelchair.'

'What? But, I saw her! She waved and…'

'Didn't you notice the chair she was in? Or the man standing behind her? Or the blanket on her lap?'

'What? No! I just saw her and smiled…' My heart did something strange all of a sudden. I don't know, but my chest tightened and I put my hand to it straight away. 'What are you saying, Ronnie? What are you saying?' I demanded.

He sighed. 'She's in the local hospice now, Emma. She hasn't long to go.'

'Ronnie! No! That can't be true! It can't! She smiled and waved and even gave me a thumbs up. She…'

'She just wanted to see one last toddler morning story time, she said. She wanted to sit back and be an observer. As she said herself, she wanted to take the experience with her, to the grave.'

'Oh my God! Oh my God! Where is she, Ronnie? I have to see her NOW!'

'Emma, Emma, sit down. She's gone. Her husband had to take her back to the hospice. He stayed beyond the half hour he was supposed to. He stayed the extra twenty minutes because she insisted upon it. She wanted to stay until the end of the story. You didn't notice, but she howled with laughter along with you and the toddlers. She loved it! She kept saying, "Emma, look at Emma! I'm so proud of her!"'

Now it was my turn to burst into tears. I mean, no one had ever…no one had ever said…no one had...

No one.

'Oh my God, Ronnie,' I managed through my hands on my face. 'Oh my God,' I kept saying through my tears. He got off his stool and came over. He rubbed my back and after a few minutes I let him hug me. I let him in. I think he may have shed a tear or two as well. We both realised we couldn't go back to the library. We risked taking the afternoon off at short notice, knowing it wouldn't go down well, but we didn't care. We couldn't concentrate. We wouldn't be able to work.

We decided we'd confront the backlash from our understaffed colleagues on Monday. We drove to the hospice but it was fruitless. Only immediate family were allowed in. I just wanted to see her. I wanted to hug her. I wanted to touch her hand and her face and tell her how much she meant to me. I wanted to let her know what a powerful influence she'd been on me in my life since I began working with her ten years ago. She had taken me under her wing and protected me and encouraged me. I wanted to tell her she was the... She was the mother I never had. There! I said it! Even though, only to myself. It was an overdue admission. It was something I'd never allowed myself to think, but now I just did.

She was not only the mother I never had, but also the mother I should have had. The kind of mother I would have thrived under. The kind of mother with whom I would have soared. The kind of mother I would have loved. With all my heart and soul. With every fibre of my being. I did love her dearly, and I think she must have known that. She had a family of her own and she shared their stories with me. How her daughter got involved with the wrong kind of guy and got pregnant too soon and he left her and refused child support. How her son went to motorcycle across America and she only gets a postcard from him every now and then. I think, in some ways, she felt she had failed her own kids and tried to make up for it in her love and care for her two grandchildren. And for me.

I felt it. I think we both did. We were kindred spirits. She was my mentor and protector. I was her second chance to get it right. We never discussed my mother at length, but she knew from my brief snippets here and there the way things were. She knew. And I knew she knew, so we didn't need to go there. That suited me just fine.

*   *   *

Myself and Ronnie went to the local park. We looked at the ducks, admired the newly planted trees and walked in silence for a good deal of it. We consoled each other with our presence. We didn't need to say anything. We were both profoundly affected by Patricia's illness in similar ways. I'm sure Patricia made Ronnie feel like the son she never had, despite having a son. He was desperately fond of her and we shared our sadness by just walking together in silence.

As our meditative ramble came to a natural end, Ronnie asked if I'd like to go to his place to meet his cat. I looked at him and smiled. 'You never mentioned your cat, Ronnie!'

'No. Or my girlfriend. But, alas, only one of them is real!' We both laughed. I loved that he could still make me laugh despite my deep sadness.

'Well, I'd better go actually. Mark gets home kind of early on a Friday. So, em, I suppose I'll never know which one is real! For some strange reason, though, I hope it's the cat,' I said.

'Oh yeah? Why?' he asked. I was glad I seemed to be able to make him happy too.

'I don't know. I just think I like the idea of you having a cat, that's all.' With that I hugged him, meaningfully, and went home to share my tragic news with Mark.

Chapter Eleven

Patricia didn't leave my mind all weekend. I didn't mention it to my mother, but I spilled my heart out to Mark. He listened and was sympathetic, but I could tell he didn't really understand. How could he? He didn't know, Patricia. He'd only met her once, briefly. The reality of it was that Ronnie was the only one who understood. I wished the weekend away, so I could get to see him again at work on Monday.

We took our break together in the afternoon and spent the whole forty-five minutes wondering whether Patricia would make another appearance in the library on Wednesday. I desperately hoped she would as I didn't get to say a proper goodbye to her. At least Ronnie had spent some time chatting to her and her husband while I was reading the story. I'd only exchanged a tiny wave with her, assuming she would stick around long enough for us to have one of our chats. Had I known she was going to be whisked away, I would have ditched the story and ran over to her. Of course when I shared this with Ronnie, he reacted strongly.

'No, no, Emma. She loved listening to the story. That was exactly what she wanted. Her husband told me so. She wasn't supposed to leave the hospice under any circumstances, but she threatened him!'

'She what?' We both laughed.

'Yeah, yeah, she threatened to haunt him from the grave if he refused!'

'Now, that is sooooo Patricia!!' We threw our heads back in hysterics.

But, later when I thought about it, I was flattered that Patricia would go to such lengths to hear me read to the toddlers. It meant something to me. She'd entrusted her lifelong beloved legacy at the library to me. I couldn't fathom why. I had shown no interest in the kids' section until recent months when she roped me in. I guess something magical had happened between me and Ronnie, and

Patricia sensed it too. On more than one occasion she referred to us as 'The Dream Team'.

She didn't appear on Tuesday. On Wednesday, myself and Ronnie busied ourselves to no end. The library had never looked so impeccable or been so ultra organised. The book displays were exemplary, the boxes in the store room were emptied and sorted, and the anti-virus software was updated ahead of schedule. We just didn't know what to do with ourselves and constant busyness was a good distraction.

Five o'clock came and she didn't come. We knew if she was coming it would more than likely be a morning visit. But the work day had passed and our shift was ending. I didn't make eye contact with Ronnie on my way out. We'd kept out of each other's way all day. We didn't even have our break together because we didn't want to consider the fact that Patricia might not come.

She didn't return.

And I never saw her again.

*　　*　　*

Patricia died peacefully in her sleep on Friday morning.

I was off duty for my mother at the weekend as Alan was home for a brief trip and said he'd stay with her. I didn't even tell her about Patricia. I feared an unsympathetic reaction and couldn't face it. I was like a log all weekend on the couch. Even Mark started getting impatient with me.

'You'll feel better tomorrow once the funeral is over and done with. You'll get a sense of closure and can say a proper goodbye to her.'

'I seriously doubt that, Mark. If anything, seeing her coffin being lowered into the ground will make me feel worse.'

'Emma, I don't know what to say. You knew she was dying. It's not like this is a shock. And, now we've wasted a whole weekend because you couldn't get off the couch.'

I stood up. 'There! I'm off the couch. Happy now?'

He looked up with shock in his eyes.

I picked up my blanket and box of tissues and announced that I was going to bed.

* * *

I sat next to Ronnie at the funeral mass. When he saw me, he smiled sadly and told me I looked bloody awful. I laughed and returned the insult. It looked like we'd had similar weekends.

The family made a huge fuss of us, telling us that Patricia never stopped talking about us and what a great team we made. It was equally heart-warming as it was heart-breaking to hear all of this. We said our goodbyes while promising to keep in touch, even though we all knew we wouldn't. Patricia was our link and now she was gone.

Ronnie and myself left Patricia's house together that evening and I can honestly say nothing was ever the same between us after that. We never realised what a magnet Patricia was, holding our little threesome together. Without her, we had no momentum. We didn't coordinate our breaks or get back to having daily belly laughs together. If anything, we were a little awkward.

Of course, we carried on the toddler mornings and kids' activities, but we shared the rota and didn't overlap, so we weren't exactly working together as a 'Dream Team', but rather opposite each other, one clocking on as the other clocked off. Independently, it seemed we'd concluded that Patricia was the glue that held us together and we couldn't seem to get our chemistry back without her.

*   *   *

However, following Patricia's sad passing and burial, I had other things on my mind. Like, for example, missing my period…for the first time in, well…coming close to thirty-nine years! With the exception of my twelve prepubescent years, that is…

Oh My God! Oh My God! What was happening? Two days had passed already and there was no sign of it. I usually menstruated like clockwork on the dot, every twenty-eight days. What was happening? I didn't want to jump to conclusions, yet I was JUMPING to CONCLUSIONS! I didn't know what to do with myself and couldn't concentrate at work, so I went off on my own for an extended lunch break on day two of my missed period period. I needed to confide in someone, so I took out my phone in the coffee shop and consulted Google.

After a half hour of Googling I felt massively deflated. Turns out a missed period at thirty-eight and three quarters years of age can mean early onset menopause. Even despite having substantial amounts of unprotected sex! Who knew? With that disappointing knowledge, I returned to work and made a beeline for the women's health section. I borrowed three books—*What to Expect When You're Not Expecting the Perimenopause, When the Menopause Simply Can't Wait for You* and *Lo and Behold! You're Not Pregnant! You're Barren!* Hmmm, I wasn't sure about the last title. Three exclamation marks in a non-fiction book title didn't fill me with confidence, but I borrowed it anyway. Maybe it would prove to be amusing and I could do with a laugh. I realised I hadn't laughed since the day of Patricia's funeral, when Ronnie told me I looked bloody awful. It made me smile to think of it, followed by feelings of guilt that I was smiling about something that happened on the day of Patricia's funeral. That made me sad again.

I got home and Mark greeted me with the news that he'd just ordered a takeaway.

'You still look miserable, Emma. When are you going to get over Patricia's death?'

Ouch! His words stung. I didn't appreciate his phrasing. He wasn't helping me out of my grief. If anything, he was contributing to it. He must have realised from my expression.

'I'm sorry, I don't mean to sound harsh. It's just, I miss you, that's all.'

Okay, that deserved a hug at least. He tried for more, but I pulled away.

'No, Mark! Not now.' I didn't mean to snap, but I wanted to give him a clear message that we wouldn't be having sex tonight.

'What's wrong with you?' He appeared startled.

'I'm just…just not feeling myself, that's all. Maybe I need an early night or something.'

He laughed. 'An early night? You've had nothing but early nights all week! I thought we could do something this weekend, like go out for a meal maybe?'

I had no such inclinations. I went into the living room, put my bags down and spread out on the couch.

'What? Am I getting the silent treatment now for asking my girlfriend to go out for dinner? Is this what's actually happening?'

'No! Chill out, Mark. I'm not ignoring you. My bags were heavy and I wanted to sit down.'

'Oh good! For a second there, I thought you were turning into your mother!' he said.

Sucker punch! How could he? How could he say something so hurtful and spiteful to me when I was at my lowest? He must have sensed from my pained expression that he'd gone too far. My eyes filled with tears and all of a sudden I was blinded by them. I pulled a tissue out of my pocket. He lifted my feet and sat down at the other end of the couch before placing my feet on his lap.

'Shit, sorry. I didn't expect that reaction. Really, I didn't mean to upset you.'

I blew my nose loudly and got a fresh tissue for my eyes.

'Yeah, it's just, I thought you knew that's a sensitive subject for me. Most people get that. I thought you did too.'

'Yeah, look, I said I was sorry, okay? Let's just forget it.' He looked down. 'So, what's in the bag? Did you go shopping or something?'

I hesitated. Should I come clean? Should I tell him? He'd probably be delighted to know we wouldn't be needing condoms anymore, now that I was starting the menopause. This would most likely make his day!

'Mark, I think I know why I've been feeling so lethargic lately.'

'Hmm? What do you mean? I thought it was because of Patricia?'

'Yes, of course, of course, but I think it's related to something else as well.'

'You're not sick, are you? Oh shit! It's nothing serious, is it?' He seemed genuinely concerned. Of course he was. I mean, I was his girlfriend after all.

'No, no, not sick. It's quite common in a woman my age actually.'

'What is?' I could see he was baffled.

'Perimenopause,' I informed him.

'The what? What?' he jumped up, dropping my feet on the couch. 'What are you talking about, Emma?'

I sat up and bent over to grab a book out of the bag. 'I don't really know exactly, but hopefully I'll gain some insights from these books.'

He looked at it. *What to Expect When You're Not Expecting...*' He trailed off. I studied him. He had a look of shock on him.

'What's wrong, Mark? It might be advantageous for you, y'know. We may not have to bother with condoms ever again!' I tried and failed to cheer him up. He opened the book and flicked through it, before reaching into the bag to look at the others.

He turned to look me in the eye. 'Who diagnosed you? I mean, when did you even go to the doctor?'

'Oh, I diagnosed my symptoms myself with the help of good old, trusty Google,' I smiled.

He looked confused. 'What symptoms? Tiredness?'

'Hmmm? Well, not just that. I'm a couple of days late, so I…'

'Late?' All of a sudden, his expression changed. 'You mean you missed a period?'

'Well, I'm unusually late, anyway,' I said.

He beamed, ear to ear, wider than I'd ever seen. 'Tired? Lethargic? Late? Emma! Let's go get you a pregnancy test!'

Chapter Twelve

I protested and told him what I'd learned from Google on my lunch break earlier that day. But he insisted that a pregnancy test was urgently required. I was too exhausted to get off the couch, but he made me.

'I'm not going into the chemist alone to buy a pregnancy test! No way! Come on! Lean on me.' He offered me his hand. 'I'll drive,' he said. I followed him downstairs to the carpark where he opened the door for me and guided me into the passenger seat.

I peered sideways at him from my vantage point. He looked like a man on a mission. He was wired. He ran a red light and everything.

'Jeez, Mark! I'm not having a baby now! Slow down!'

He laughed and looked at me. 'No, not now, but you might be in nine months!' He had a massive grin planted on his face. I turned in my seat to look out the window. I needed to check in with myself to see how I felt. For starters, definitely not as excited as Mark. I'd always been unsure about whether I wanted to have a baby or not. I'd thought about it and mentioned I would, but I always imagined it would be some time in the far off future when I was mature and responsible—some time in the imaginary future when I was 'ready'. I knew of so many others around my age who were desperate to have one, like Helen and Julia. I could never identify with the strength of their urges. My urge was hovering in the background. Theirs was a powerful force, determining every decision they made in their late thirties. It would almost seem unfair if I was pregnant, given I wasn't trying as hard as them. Then, Mark started singing 'The Wheels on the Bus' and I realised he was—he was TRYING to become a father since the day he met me.

I scooched around on my seat, feeling slightly on edge. He made no bones about admitting that he wanted to have a family. I wondered why it didn't work out with Julia, given it seemed as though they both wanted exactly the same thing. But he wasn't good-looking enough for her and I don't know, I think she thought him 'bland'. I'm pretty sure he saw me as the maternal sort from the moment he met me. Probably because I was caring, a good daughter and an all-round good person in general, I think. But that didn't mean I'd have a hankering to become a mom. It just meant I cared about others. Maybe even more so than I cared for myself. *I don't know, I suppose that's the making of decent parent material.*

He came around, offering me his hand to help me out of the car. 'Mark, stop with this! It's too much, really!' I found it a little embarrassing.

I picked the first pregnancy test I saw and Mark picked up two more. 'What are you doing?' I asked. 'Sometimes you get a false reading on the first one, so it's worthwhile to have backups,' he replied.

'Oh,' I said, remembering he'd been through all of this before with his previous girlfriend, Ger. He seemed as though he had high hopes for me. I supposed my pear-shaped body lent itself to the notion of childbearing hips. We'd soon find out, I guess.

*   *   *

'I knew it! I knew it, Emma!' he exclaimed before breaking down in tears. He bawled while I examined the test result and read and reread the instructions. He was on the floor now, overcome with emotion. I didn't know how I felt.

'Emma!' He looked up at me and grabbed my hand. 'I love you.'

I stood there and let him squeeze my hand. I wasn't sure what was happening. He stood up and embraced me, resting his head on my shoulder. I could feel my blouse getting wet from his tears. It was soaking into my bra strap. He sniffed. Now I was confused as to whether it was just his tears or more than that seeping through my clothes. I was a little troubled that he didn't think to get a tissue and was effectively wiping his nose on my clothes. That was the overriding feeling I had on finding out I was going to become a mother—one of discomfort.

I pulled away. 'Here, let me get you a tissue,' I said.

'Oh thanks. Thanks, love,' he sniffed, wiping his nose with his hand. I handed him the tissue and he blew his nose and wiped his eyes. 'Let's sit down and take this in,' he said.

'Aren't you going to wash your hands after the…' I checked.

'Oh, sure, yeah. I'll be back!' he beamed.

Why did the fact that he was so overwhelmed with emotion bother me?

He reappeared. 'Shit!' he shouted. I jumped. 'What is it?' I asked, alarmed.

'We must have missed the takeaway delivery while we were at the pharmacy. Damn it!'

'Oh, is that all?' I felt my shoulders dropping as I melted into the couch.

'Honey, can I get you anything? Are you hungry? There's soup in the fridge.'

'Hmmm? Oh, well, maybe that's what's wrong with me,' I decided. I was probably hungry. He heated some soup and made toast. I joined him at the table and we ate. We were starving.

'Much healthier than a takeaway!' I announced.

He nodded. He'd been studying me. 'Emma, are you excited? You seem a bit muted.'

'Oh, yeah, it's a lot to take in, isn't it? I don't know yet how I'm feeling, but I know I was hungry.' The food seemed to bring some life into me.

'Of course! You're eating for two now!' he smiled. 'We'd better get you to a doctor first thing in the morning, okay?'

'Oh, my doctor doesn't do weekend surgery. It's Monday to Friday only.'

'Oh, right, mine too. Let's Google.' After a minute or two, he looked it up. 'There's a GP clinic on the MacMillan road. It says here they open the first Saturday of every month for an out of hours clinic. Let's go there. With no appointment, we'll have to get there early, okay?'

*   *   *

A very young-looking, very hungover junior doctor confirmed my pregnancy at 8.30am the next morning. I needed this confirmation. I had lain awake half the night, thinking I can't be. *This can't be real.* How could a pregnancy occur so late in my thirties without much effort on my part? I didn't deserve this. It wasn't right. People like me didn't deserve happiness like this.

But Doctor Seán Dempsey thought otherwise. 'Congratulations! You're pregnant! Here's your referral to the maternity hospital. Ring them on Monday to get an appointment.'

His innocent, warm, radiant smile made me smile too and I looked towards Mark. 'I love you,' he whispered. I looked back at the doctor's piercing blue eyes and smiled at him again. I spotted the open pack of Polo mints on his table and guessed he'd been trying to cover up the whiff of stale beer. It didn't work. The smell was pungent and his eyes were watering with tiredness. Had he slept last night? I smiled wider. I didn't care. He was lovely and gave me nothing but good news. I'd go back to my regular doctor anyway for my check-ups from here on. We stood up, shook his hand and left.

I was starting to feel excited. Now that I knew it was real. And Mark was on cloud nine. For the first time since hearing the news, I reached for him. I grabbed his hand. We could do this. We could be parents. Like normal people. We could raise this child growing in my tummy. I didn't think I could do it alone. I needed him. He seemed to know what to do. And I hadn't a clue.

He started to be a lot more attentive towards me. Mostly, I liked it, except when I was tired. I found it a bit annoying. We didn't share our news with anyone. We decided to wait for the twelve-week scan.

My mother pulled out of me the same as ever and demanded to be brought to mass, the chiropodist, shopping centres which were far away, and to friends' houses for this, that or the other. Mark was surprised at how much I actually did for her, considering she was in the whole of her health. I was grateful he offered to chip in. It was wonderful to have his support and I noticed my mother was less unkind towards me when he was around. He was like a buffer between us, even though he didn't realise it. He did suggest I should say *'no'* more often, but I figured I'd better help her out now while I could. I simply wouldn't be able to do much for her once my baby made an appearance into this world.

He made excuses every so often about why we couldn't collect her, and she didn't react. Normally, she'd turn against me if I refused her anything, but having Mark on my side felt like protection.

* * *

At the library, the toddler mornings continued to be hugely successful and well attended, despite the passing of its founder, Patricia. Myself and Ronnie gave our all to make it a success in her honour. Although we no longer took our breaks together, we did get together every

Wednesday to prepare for kids' activities, reserve suitable workshops and choose our materials for the toddler mornings. We had great fun in that hour, as Ronnie would practise his songs with me and I'd do a toddler dance in response. Then, I'd pretend to be a character in whatever book I'd chosen and stay in role for as long as I could before splitting my sides with laughter.

Neither of us mentioned why we didn't seem to schedule our lunch breaks together. It would be great as we used to have so much fun, but I think we felt awkward about arranging lunch for two. It was more of a get together between pals when it was the three of us, but now that Patricia was gone, there would be a sad emptiness at the table. I figured we were both trying to avoid that heartbreaking void. No amount of lunchtime banter could fill that hole.

I missed talking to Ronnie at my lunch breaks. I missed sharing EVERYTHING with Patricia. I would definitely have shared my pregnancy news with her ahead of the twelve-week scan. I knew she would have given me so much advice and made sure I wasn't doing any heavy lifting at work. I was still in touch with Julia. She was going ninety on the Dublin dating scene and even taking the odd trip to Galway and Cork to check out the single men there. Neither of us heard much from Helen in the UK anymore, but last we'd heard was that her latest romance was going strong.

I thought about sharing my baby news with Julia, but she never really asked about Mark. It was as though she didn't want to admit that I was in a serious relationship and she wasn't. I knew if the tables were turned, I'd do my utmost to be supportive of her and try to be happy for her, even if I felt like I was getting left behind. Out of the three of us, I think I was the one who wanted marriage and family the least, and now it seemed I was closest to both.

Mark's devotion since the pregnancy news overwhelmed me. Mostly in a good way. He was doing everything for me—cooking, hoovering, shopping. He even took a half day to fix the tap in the bathroom and replace one or two wonky cupboard doors. He accompanied me and my mother to visit her friend Bernadette at the weekend, where he spotted a house for sale in the neighbourhood of Cedarwood Drive. He was taken with the area and mentioned on a few occasions how it would be a prime location to raise a family. He booked a viewing with the estate agent. He said he'd go first and if he thought it was worth it, I could go along for the second viewing.

I'd never really imagined leaving my two-bedroomed apartment, but now that Mark pointed out so many un-child-friendly aspects, such as the prospect of climbing two flights of stairs with a buggy, or the lack of garden space, I began to agree that we needed to find a house with a garden. Somewhere located near good schools and a park with a playground. I started checking the MyHome website and finding affordable homes, but they were all miles away. The house Mark wanted to view was way out of budget and much too big for what we would actually need. It had three bedrooms and a converted attic, along with a living room, playroom, extended kitchen and large, grassy back garden. I mean, I could see it working for a family of five, but we would only be three. That's when I wondered if Mark had more ambitious plans than me for our future family. I decided to quiz him.

'So, this house you're viewing in Cedarwood Drive, it's…'

'I know, Emma, it's amazing, isn't it? It's just what we…'

'Yeah, it's a great house, I agree. But it's so expensive, and don't you think it's a little bigger than what we'd actually need? I mean, there'll only be three of us and…'

'You don't know that, Emma.'

'What? What do you mean? I do know! There's one baby in my tummy, not twins. Only one heartbeat was detected at my last appointment and…'

'I know that, but, like, you never know, in the future, we might…'

'No.'

'What?'

'No. I won't be having anymore.'

'Emma! What's wrong? This is not like you at all!'

'What do you mean? I'm just telling you that this will be my one and only pregnancy.'

'One child doesn't make a family. We'll have more! Now that we know we can!'

'Mark, this wasn't my plan, you know. I wanted to meet someone and then maybe one day have a baby, when the time was right. But this is all happening so quickly. I didn't think it would and…'

'Yeah, it's great it's happening so fast. It means we can go on to have more than one, maybe two or three, a proper family.'

'Three? Mark! I don't even know if I'm ready to have one!'

'Yes! Yes, you are! I knew it the minute I met you. You were born to be a mother. I could tell from your personality and your clothes and your warm smile…'

'My clothes?'

'Yes. You were wearing that long, mustard cardigan under your blue coat and I thought…'

'What?'

'Well, it looked kind of…maternal. A bit like something my mum used to wear in the seventies,' he informed me with a big grin on his face.

I was stunned. That made me feel weird. I thought he fancied me when he first met me, but now I find out I reminded him of his mother. This was not good. Definitely not what I wanted to hear. I feigned tiredness, brushed him on the cheek and went to bed, thinking how much a new wardrobe of fashionable, non-mumsie clothes was urgently required.

Chapter Thirteen

He fell in love with the house, from the doorknob to the kitchen sink! And, damn it, so did I. The minute I stepped through the front door, I could imagine a baby crawling around on the soft carpet in the hall. The sellers obviously had small children, because the playroom was decked out with a wall-mounted Barbie house, floor-to-ceiling toy shelves and a bean bag couch. Seemingly, they were loath to sell such a beautiful family home, but the parents were artists and got offered a once-in-a-lifetime opportunity to work in New Zealand on a project close to their hearts, so they were selling up.

Mark grabbed my hand as we surveyed the American-style double door fridge freezer. However, the back garden was what won us over ultimately. It was at least twenty metres long, with a tree house, a swingset and a trampoline that the current owners would be leaving behind. It was perfect and for the first time, I started visualising what the future could hold for me. I could see my baby on a bucket seat on the swing, or discovering the treehouse for the first time or crawling under the trampoline until they were big enough to bounce on it. My heart filled with feelings of inexpressible joy and excitement, until Mark brought me back to earth and showed me the sales brochure.

Now we were on a mission. We couldn't get the house out of our minds and it was all we talked about over breakfast, lunch and dinner. I had thought it was out of our budget initially, but Mark, being a banker, insisted we could afford it if we stretched to our maximum affordability levels. He said it would be our house for life. Strangely, I flinched when he said that. He noticed.

'What's wrong? You're not a commitment-phobe or something, are you?'

'Hmm? No. It's just, 'for life'. Those are scary words.'

'I think I know what this is about,' he announced. Did he? I didn't know what this was about. My sudden, reflex flinch action surprised even me. I looked at him, wide-eyed, waiting for him to shed some light.

'You want that ring on your finger first, don't you? Before we start pooling our resources and investing in property, you want to make it official, don't you? I know what women want, even if they're scared to admit it themselves,' he said with an all-knowing look. One which sent a shiver up my spine. I didn't respond initially. How could he know me so little? Considering we were starting a family together and everything. How could he come out with comments like that? I thought about it for a few minutes, before formulating my question for him.

'Mark, what was your last girlfriend like? Ger—tell me about her.'

'Hmm?' He looked surprised. He wasn't expecting that. 'Why? Why do you want to know about her?'

'I don't know. I think it might just help me understand you more. I mean, you said you were together nearly ten years and hoping to start a family. So, she was a major part of your life for a long time and you were engaged, weren't you? I'd just like to know a little about her, that's all. I think that's a perfectly reasonable thing to ask the father of your future baby, don't you?'

He sat back and shrugged. 'Oh. Okay, well if you really want to know, she was, em, quite different to you, in appearance, like, well, and more than that. In other ways too.'

I'd never seen him fumble for words like this. He ran his hands through his dark hair. I always thought it looked too dark for his complexion anyway, making him look pale. It looked like a colour from a bottle that a middle-aged man desperate to defy ageing would naively massage onto his scalp, without checking whether it matched his skin tone first. But it actually wasn't. It was his natural hair colour and although he was in his early forties, he had not got one grey hair.

'She was glamorous, you know, liked to dress up in high heels and the latest fashion. She was well up with what was currently trending.' *Okay, sounds like she IS the opposite of me. A librarian who likes comfortable shoes and woolly cardigans.* I wouldn't know what was currently trending if it hit me in the face. Unless it was a book.

'And, eh, she liked the finer things. You know, she wanted the best of this and that, she had expensive tastes.' He caught my eyes and I tried to remain neutral. 'I like that you don't,' he said, attempting reassurance. 'Hmm,' I said, 'but what was she like? You know, her personality?'

'Oh yeah, she was funny,' he chuckled. 'I used to laugh at her crazy notions sometimes. She had unrealistic expectations. I often had to bring her down, back to reality. She wasn't as…sensitive as you, Emma. She could be a bit cutting, but I could handle it. She...I mean we desperately wanted to have a baby. It took over and, at the end of the day, it ruined our relationship. We couldn't get it back. Whatever it was that we had, we couldn't relight it after so many failed pregnancies and disappointments. She met someone after we broke up.' He sank deeper into the couch and looked towards the ceiling as if he was talking to himself. 'She would have loved the house we…' He stopped himself. He checked in, before continuing. 'She had, em, expensive taste, as I said.' He got up, went into the kitchen and came back with a beer.

I noted he didn't ask me if I wanted anything from the fridge. I got up and poured myself a sparkling water. The heat was getting to me. When I returned, he had the TV on and his beer was half empty. He didn't look my way, so I whispered a half-hearted goodnight and went to bed early.

* * *

The next morning was Saturday and I realised my mother had not yet rung me with her agenda for the weekend. She usually got me on a Friday evening as soon as I got home from work, but I had no missed calls and I forgot to ring her.

I made some bacon and eggs. Mark was sleeping in. I didn't hear him coming to bed last night, so it must have been late. He'd had a fair few beers. Reminiscing about his ex seemed to increase his thirst. I guess it was my fault. I probably should never have brought it up. It was just that marriage comment. It seemed as though it should have been directed at someone else, not me. Because I wasn't waiting for him to propose. I was still trying to get my head around the fact that, a) I had a boyfriend, and b) I was growing a baby in my tummy. Not to mention the prospect of selling my hard-won apartment and committing my life savings to a family home in the suburbs. This was enough for me. The idea of marriage had not entered my mind for one second. It really felt like he was confusing me with someone else. And from the sounds of what he told me last night, maybe he was getting me mixed up with Ger and assuming I wanted the same things as her. I didn't know. I worried sometimes about how little we really knew each other, considering the humongous life steps we were taking together as a couple. It frightened me on occasion when I thought about it, but I motored on and boiled the kettle for a pot of tea, before giving him a shout that breakfast was ready.

I phoned my mother after breakfast but got no response. That was strange. She'd normally have a list ready for me by this time on a Saturday morning. I was glad of the break, but also concerned that I hadn't heard from her. I tried calling again. Mark told me to take a well-earned rest from her. He was getting sick of her constant demands and requested a weekend off. He wanted to do some more work on our finances to ensure the offer we were proposing for the house would be affordable for us. He was looking up maternity leave entitlements for state librarians because I told him I hadn't a clue what I was entitled to.

I tried to put my mind to other things, but kept coming back to why my mother hadn't responded to my calls. I told Mark I was going to pick up his dry cleaning and might pop to the shops too. He saw right through me, though.

'You're going to check on Angela, aren't you? She's got some hold over you. You're constantly at her beck and call. The library must be like a break for you and that's your full-time employment.'

'Hmm, well, yeah, I guess I'm lucky that I love my job so much, so yes, it is kind of a break to go there Monday to Friday,' I beamed, considering myself one of the lucky ones. Not many people could say that about their job. At least, I really did LOVE it when Patricia greeted me every morning. I was a bit lonely without her these days, but my growing bump was a great distraction from the grief I still felt. Things were changing and moving so fast. I thought about visiting Patricia's grave and having a word with her there. I knew if she were alive she'd have plenty of wisdom to share with me regarding being pregnant, maternity leave and buying a house. She'd have good relationship advice for me too. Not that I needed it. Did I need it? I'd definitely like to talk things through with someone other than Mark. Maybe I'd give Julia a call, I decided, as I drove over to my mother's house. I glanced at my phone. Still no calls or messages from her. Something was up—that was abundantly clear.

Chapter Fourteen

There was no answer. I peered through the gap at the side of the garage and saw that her car was there. This was not right. Why wasn't she answering the door or her phone? I went back to my car to retrieve the spare key I had for her house. The porch was unlocked, but when I put the key in the front door, I couldn't open it. It unlocked, but wouldn't open. It was then I heard a groan.

'Mother? Mother? Are you there?' I started to panic. I heard more moaning and realised she was the heavy weight on the floor preventing the door from opening. 'Oh my God, oh my God,' I kept repeating, before reaching for my phone to call an ambulance. I needed help. She was on the floor and there was no way I could get to her. I called to her and told her help was on its way, but there was very little response from her.

The paramedics arrived and faced the same difficulties as me regarding gaining entry. They said if she were responsive, they would be able to guide her so she would slide or roll when the door opened, but she couldn't follow instructions in her current state. The local guards had to be called. They broke in through the sitting room window at the front of the house and let the paramedics in that way. At this stage, the neighbours were out in their droves, wondering what had happened to Angela.

The ambulance team worked their magic at an unbelievable pace and brought her out on a stretcher. They informed me it looked as though she fell down the stairs and were fairly certain her left hip was broken. She'd also sustained other injuries including a bump to the head, which meant she was in and out of consciousness. She needed to be treated immediately and told me to follow the ambulance in my car. Because medical attention was urgently required, there was no room for me in the ambulance.

I stood there and listened attentively, trying to take in every shred of valuable information they imparted, but as soon as they drove away, I realised I was still standing there with absolutely no clue what to do. Luckily, the neighbours rushed to my aid. Nora offered to lock up the house and keep an eye on it while Angela was in hospital. Liam from across the road checked my tyres and had a quick look at my engine. I had no idea why. Rose brought me inside and made me a cup of tea to bring colour back to my face.

'You need your wits about you to drive to the hospital. It's a busy road. Here, drink this,' she said. As I sipped the strong, hot, just-the-right-shade-of-brown liquid, I remembered that Mother would need an overnight bag. Her things. I must pack a bag for her with her things in it. I thanked Rose for the heavenly cuppa and ran upstairs. I got her nightie, dressing gown, toothbrush, toothpaste and slippers. That would do for tonight. I could come back tomorrow to get more.

With that, I thanked everyone and dashed to the hospital. I went straight to A&E and asked for the whereabouts of Angela Ward.

'Yes, I'm her next of kin,' I said. 'Her daughter.'

'Oh,' said the receptionist. 'She asked for her son.'

'Pardon me?' I asked.

'As she was being wheeled in, I asked her who her next of kin was and she said "My son, my son". Is it Alan? I couldn't quite make it out. They were in an awful hurry.'

Everything in my upper body sank to the lowest part of my tummy and this inhibited my breathing. I took a moment. 'Yes, my brother, Alan, but he's in the UK. I'm her daughter.'

'Oh, I see. We have to be careful. I'm sorry. You do understand, don't you?'

Oh gosh, the poor woman must have seen the colour drain from my face. Apologising to me…I mean, really, there was no need. She was just doing her job.

'Yes, yes, of course,' I tried to reassure her.

'Your name?'

'My what? Oh, right, yes, I'm my mother's daughter and my name is Emma.' I felt faint. I held onto the counter to steady myself.

'Emma?' she asked.

'Yes, Emma,' I replied.

'Sorry, Emma, I need your surname.'

'Ward.'

'Oh, your mother's in Ward 7. I'll show you in a minute.'

'Hmmm?' I asked.

'Em, your surname, please?'

'War...' And that was when I fell to the floor. The porter rushed to my aid and helped me up. I just lost consciousness for a few seconds. He sat me down and brought me some water. A passing nurse advised me to put my head down between my knees, so I did. I stayed like that for a few minutes, feeling the blood flow to my brain. I didn't realise I was on my own. When I sat up, it was clear the nurse and porter were only passing by. Of course they were. This was a hospital, a busy place. They couldn't be wasting their time looking after me, nothing but a visitor, a blow-in. They had patients with serious injuries and illnesses to attend to. I sat there feeling like a fool. When I looked towards the reception desk, I saw a massive queue had formed. Oh well, you snooze, you lose. I got up, picked up the bag of my mother's belongings that the porter must have carried over for me, and waited at the end of the line.

I rang Mark to let him know where I was.

'You're at the hospital? Oh my God, are you…? Is the baby…?' That's when it dawned on me that I was pregnant. I had forgotten. Maybe my fainting had something to do with that. Should I be concerned? I'd think about that later.

'Yes, no, Mark, I'm here because my mother had an accident.'

'Oh thank God!' he said.

'Mark?'

'Oh sorry, Emma, I didn't mean that. I'm just glad you and the baby are okay.'

I filled him in on the details of my mother's accident and explained I could be there for a while as I hadn't even seen her yet. I didn't mention the fainting. He'd worry too much and I was actually grand. Not a bother on me now. I was just very hungry, that was all.

By the time I got to the top of the queue there was a different receptionist on duty, so we began again. She told me my mother was in Ward 7, Cubicle 1. She rang to check if I was allowed in. Nobody picked up so she told me to take a seat in the waiting area and she'd let me know. I began to ask her if there was anywhere nearby I could get a sandwich but she'd already moved on to the next person in line. Maybe she didn't hear me through the glass partition.

I sat down and listened to my rumbling tummy. Nobody came and I didn't manage to make eye contact with the receptionist. I was trying to remind her that I was still waiting. I wasn't in her direct eyeline and there was nobody around to ask. I waited until the line got smaller and joined the queue again. She recognised me. 'Oh yes,' she said, 'I'll try again. It's so busy in there.'

'I understand,' I said. I did. I understood. This was a hospital. A manic place. It was times like this that I appreciated my job in the library. A calmer existence, where we were kept steadily busy, but our tasks lacked the urgency of those that the hospital tasks required.

She got through and told me where to go. It was like a maze. The corridors were so long and the signs didn't correspond with the receptionist's directions. I had to stop and check with a security officer. He set me on the right path and I eventually reached Ward 7. The curtain was closed around Cubicle 1. I froze, wondering what kind of shape my mother would be in. They told me she bumped her head. Would she be bandaged? Bloodied? Would she even be recognizable to me? And a broken hip in a woman of her age. Is this something she could recover from? Would she ever walk again? A nurse interrupted my thoughts of doom.

'Can I help you? Who are you here for?' she asked, kindly.

'My…my mother.' I pointed towards Cubicle 1.

She smiled and led the way, opening the curtain. 'Angela!' she said, with genuine excitement in her voice. 'Look who's here!'

Mother was lying down with her head propped up on pillows. The blanket was pulled up around her shoulders. She wasn't bloodied or bandaged or even ruffled looking. She turned her head. 'Mmm,' she mumbled, acknowledging the anticlimax of my presence. Of my existence, maybe. I wasn't expecting her to look like herself. I thought she'd look more like a hospital patient, since that's exactly what she was. I'd expected her to look vulnerable. But she didn't. She looked like herself.

'Hi, I, em, brought you some things. I, em, how are you?' I struggled to release words. The nurse thought it might be shock and attempted to break the ice.

'Oh, you're quick off the mark! An overnight bag already! Well done! She'll need that. Angela's going to be here for quite some time until that hip fracture mends itself, aren't you, Angela?'

Mother blinked and nodded. The nurse smiled and turned to me. 'She'll be admitted into St Joseph's Ward on the seventh floor. A bed just became available and they're preparing it now. The doctor has already spoken to Angela about the next step but she's on heavy medication for the pain, so it mightn't have sunk in. I'll tell the doctor you're here and she'll go through everything with you. But don't worry, your mother is going to be just fine!'

She pulled over a chair for me by her bedside. 'Now, I'll leave you two in peace. Have a lovely chat and I'll get the doctor to brief you with the prognosis as soon as she's ready.' I couldn't help smiling back. The nurse had such a warm, compassionate smile. She was made for a caring profession such as this. I sat down and looked at my mother.

'Are you comfortable? Can I…' She waved her hand and I took that to mean she was okay as she was.

'So, do you remember what happened? How did you fall?'

'I was coming downstairs to ring you to tell you about the weeds in the driveway,' she informed me. 'But I never made it to my phone. I must have tripped on the third or fourth step from the bottom. I remember lying there and not being able to move. I got some bang and a knock to the head.' She felt the bump under her hair on the left side of her head.

'Oh gosh, that must have been terrible, not being able to move?'

'I couldn't get up. I tried, but the pain was too much. They told me I probably made things worse by trying to move. Then I heard my phone ringing but couldn't get to it. I shouted for a while, wondering if the neighbours would hear me, but nobody came.'

'That was me ringing, I bet. I tried again this morning.'

'I didn't hear it. I think I eventually fell asleep or passed out. Next thing I know, they're lifting me onto a stretcher and telling me my hip is broken.'

'Can you feel any pain now?'

'No, they have me dosed up well and good.' She yawned.

'They do. Have a rest now. I'll go and ask if I can bring your bag up to the ward. It's great you got a bed so soon. I've heard stories about people being left in cubicles in A&E, on trolleys even, and…' I stopped. I think she'd fallen asleep. My phone beeped so I left her bedside, not wanting to wake her. It was Mark asking if I was still waiting and offering to take over or bring me in some food. I smiled to myself. It felt good to have someone looking after me like this. He really cared. He loved me. I told him I'd be home soon and went to find the doctor to get the lowdown.

Chapter Fifteen

The days and weeks that followed saw my mother have a successful hip operation and my tummy swell into a rotund baby bump. The 12-week scan told us our baby was healthy and well with a strong heartbeat. I cried. Mark cried. We were a mess, but a blissful one.

We could tell people now. The first person I told was my brother, Alan. He was over the moon for me. And Mark. I mean for us, both of us. He passed the phone on to Sophie. She asked me one hundred million questions, which told me she definitely wanted to have a baby some day. She promised me they'd be home in advance of my due date and offered to help with buggy shopping, baby names and potential venues for the christening party. I'd barely considered any of those necessities, so I told her I urgently required her assistance as soon as she could make it back to Ireland.

Next, I rang Julia. Her reaction was muted. 'Congrats,' she said. 'When are you due?' And then she changed the subject to tell me about her upcoming holiday to visit Helen in the UK. I wished her well and told her I was delighted she was getting away for the long weekend. I told her boring old me was doing nothing exciting for the bank holiday, except visiting my mother in hospital. My mother—she was the next person I told.

'I thought you two were plotting something,' she said.

I laughed, wondering if she'd just made a joke, but her expression informed me I was wrong.

'What do you mean?' I pleaded.

'What a time to announce you're pregnant! For starters, you're not married. How am I supposed to explain this to my friends and our relations? And secondly, you're having a baby while your mother is laid up in hospital, unable to walk or do a damn thing for herself. Who the hell is going to look after me? They said I could go home in a couple of weeks, but I'll need to be looked after.'

'Did they? Two weeks? But you're not mobile yet. I thought you'd be getting some physio first and then…'

'The physio will come to my house and work with me there. They need the hospital bed, Emma. You know how it is.'

'Yes, yes, I suppose I do. They're always so busy here, aren't they?'

'They need my bed for some other poor unfortunate. They'll discharge me in two weeks if I've someone to look after me while I'm learning to walk again.'

'Oh, so do we need to organise a carer or something?' I asked.

'Well, that's more for people who don't have any family nearby, isn't it?'

'What do you mean?' I wasn't sure where she was going with this.

'Well, you know Maura down the road from me? Her daughter pops over every morning to help get her up and dressed and...'

'Her daughter, Liz, who lives across the road? The one whose youngest child moved out last year to go to college and she took early retirement and now doesn't know what to do with herself?'

'Yes. Liz. She's great. She can't do enough for her mother, you know. We should have her around for tea some day. She's a saint.'

'We?' I wondered, aloud.

'Yes, well I've plenty of room, you know that. And sure it would only be a temporary measure while I get back on my feet. A few weeks, max. The physio thinks I'm making great progress and...'

'What about Mark?'

'Oh, couldn't he mind your apartment for you? Maybe even give it a lick of paint while you stay with me for a week or two. Wouldn't he be delighted to have the place to himself?'

'No. No, he'd hate that. He wants to look after me, especially now that I'm...well, pregnant...with his baby.' My voice sort of trailed off. I think I was in shock. This was a lot to take on. I instinctively placed my hand on my expanding belly and rubbed it in circular motions. It comforted me and hopefully my baby too.

'Well, think about it. If you can make a small sacrifice for a week or two until I'm up and about. That's all I'm asking.' She waved her hands as if it was a tiny request. I'd need to process it. The whole conversation we'd just had. I needed to replay it in my head on the way home if I could remember it. I couldn't. I nearly crashed the car in fact, because I couldn't concentrate. I felt confused and baffled. I got home and Mark welcomed me with a hug. It didn't comfort me. I didn't know why, but his hugs never did. They just seemed to make me feel trapped. I was always eager for the hug to end ASAP. He didn't seem to notice, though. I was glad of that. I wouldn't want to hurt his feelings because of my intimacy issues.

'She wants what?' He looked bewildered.

'Look, it would only be for a week or two. Until she's back on her feet, that's all.'

'But, Emma, what if she needs support with walking, getting out of bed, standing up? You won't be able to take that on. You can't be doing any heavy lifting in your condition. This is your first pregnancy. You have to rest and look after yourself, not an incapacitated, immobile, elderly person.'

I inhaled. Gosh, he was right. Everything he said made perfect sense, but yet, I felt I couldn't let my mother down. She was only asking for a small sacrifice. She said it herself. He continued.

'Did you tell her we were expecting?'

'Em, yes. Yes, I think I did,' I answered, trying hard to remember.

'You think? Did you or didn't you?'

'Yes. Yes, I did. I remember now. Sorry, I'm very tired.'

'Here, sit down. I'll fix you something to eat.' He came back with a salad and crusty roll and placed it on the coffee table beside the couch.

'Well, well, well, what did Angela have to say for herself when she heard you were expecting her first grandchild?'

I picked up the roll and tore it in half. 'Hmm?' I asked.

'Did she try to leap out of the bed with excitement, did she?'

'Oh. Oh no, that's not really her style, you know that. No, she's very practical. She doesn't get excited about things like this.'

'Bizarre, isn't it? My mum danced around the kitchen when I told her. And you saw my dad's reaction, didn't you? The news nearly brought on another heart attack. They couldn't be happier though. We'll have babysitters in them, don't you worry about that.'

'Gosh, babysitters, I never thought about that. So much to organise, isn't there?'

'Eat your salad. Don't worry, we've plenty of time to think about things like that. You just look after yourself for now. Get plenty of rest and healthy food. We'll figure it all out, don't worry.'

'Thanks Mark.' He said everything I needed to hear just then. I was truly wiped. I lay back on the couch after the salad and fell asleep.

*　　*　　*

A few days later, Mark surprised me with the news that we'd just gone sale agreed on that house in Cedarwood Drive. He was ecstatic.

'So, now you see, you don't have to leave to live with your mother. She can come and stay with us in our new house for a couple of weeks until she gets better!'

'So soon? But it can't be that quick, can it? Surely, this will take a few weeks at least?'

'I'm getting it snagged next Thursday and surveyed at the weekend. If all goes well, we are free to move in the week after! It might coincide nicely with Angela getting out of hospital in fact! And then I'd be there too to help her in and out of her chair and bed and so on. You won't have to do any heavy lifting. We're not putting you at risk.'

'But, Mark, how could we go sale agreed? We haven't even put our apartments on the market yet? How can we afford…?'

'Mine went for a quick sale. Just got the call an hour ago. It's gone. Maybe I could have gotten more for it if I'd waited longer, but I didn't want to risk losing our dream home!'

'Our…dream…home? I still don't get how we could afford it with just the sale of your…'

'Look, don't worry about it. My parents lent us some money to help out. I told them we'd pay them back as soon as your apartment got sold. This will make a killing in the current climate. A two-bedroomed apartment in this location… You did well, Emma. A great buy.'

'Yeah, I love my apartment. But your parents? How much do we owe them?'

'Look, don't worry. They're not going anywhere. They're over the moon for us. They're shouting from the rooftops that they're going to be grandparents soon. We'll pay them what we can with the sale of your apartment and work hard to maintain the mortgage on the house. It'll all work out. Trust me,' he smiled.

I had to lie down. I went to my comfy spot on the couch. I felt at a loss for words. Things that directly affected my life, my world, my wellbeing and my finances were changing all around me and I seemed to have no control over any of it. I placed my hand on my tummy and reassured my baby. This was the one precious thing I wouldn't let anyone else control. He or she would be mine. And Mark's, of course. But I would have a say in their upbringing. I'd insist on my voice being heard. I struggled to do it for myself, but I would roar like a lioness for my little baby. I smiled and continued rubbing my tummy in circular motions. I felt a flutter. It made me jump. I felt it again before realising what it was. He or she was kicking. They were communicating with me. My body was filled with love. A love I'd never felt before. A love I'd only ever share between me and my baby. I imagined it was probably unconditional love. It felt wonderful.

I basked in it for a few minutes before letting Mark know that the baby kicked. He put his hand, ear and face to my tummy, but couldn't feel anything. 'Ah, must be sleeping now,' I said.

'Next time, call me straight away, okay, Emma? Straight away!'

'Okay Mark,' I said and drifted off to dreamland on the couch.

Chapter Sixteen

At four and a half months, halfway through my pregnancy, my bump was starting to become noticeable underneath my loose clothing. There was no hiding it, so I came out to my colleagues. They were thrilled for me and their congratulations gave me a spring in my step for the whole week. Ronnie was off on annual leave, so I decided to text him.

Emma
Hi, hope you're enjoying your week off. How about joining me for lunch on Monday?

Ronnie
You bet! Look forward to it ;-)

I spotted him in the library from a distance on Monday morning. I almost didn't recognise him at first, as he looked so dapper. He'd started wearing blazers and jeans instead of big woolly jumpers, and his current shape resembled that of Gary Barlow in his prime. I could see him making it work as a tribute act. There was a resemblance and I knew he definitely had the voice. I just wasn't sure if there was a massive demand for a GB tribute act in the current climate. Personally, I'd be interested for definite. I loved his music and even the solo stuff too. But then, I guess I wasn't exactly au fait with modern trends, or 'down with the kids', as they say.

He waved over and made the one o'clock sign. I responded with a thumbs up. I was looking forward to hearing what he got up to during his week off. It made me imagine my upcoming time off in a few months when my maternity leave would kick in. I couldn't wait for the change of scene. I'd never been away from the library for more than two weeks at a time, so six months off would be like a holiday of a lifetime. Of course, a newborn baby would keep me busy, no doubt. I wondered if I'd even have time to miss the library at all.

At one o'clock, I went straight to our usual haunt that we used to go to with Patricia. I didn't feel as sad as I thought I would on returning. Maybe it had something to do with all the good stuff I was about to share with Ronnie.

He was already there. I sat down opposite him. 'Hey!' he greeted me. 'Hi!' I said, eager to share all my exciting news. 'So, how was your week off?' I asked first of all.

'Amazing! It's good to get away, isn't it?'

'Absolutely! I've already forgotten the last time I took more than two days off in a row!'

'Yeah, I ended up going surfing in Lahinch with a few old mates from school. It took me a full week of lessons, but I eventually got the hang of it!'

'Oh, brilliant! I've never tried, but I imagine it's difficult to balance.' We smiled at each other and he nodded. We tucked into our toasties and sipped some coffee.

'So,' he said. 'How was your week, Emma?'

I smiled, stood up and pulled my loose chiffon blouse close to my bulging belly, to show off my bump. I waited for his reaction. It took him a few seconds, until realisation hit.

'Oh! Is that what I think it is?' he asked, but not with the excitement I'd expected. Patricia would have been dancing on table tops by now. But I guess Ronnie was a guy and I shouldn't expect the same reaction from him.

'Yes! It is! There's a baby in there!' I pointed and beamed wildly.

He looked down. I couldn't see his face. He mumbled, 'Congratulations Emma, that's great for you and Mark.' I waited, but nothing more came. Oh, how anticlimactic. I felt like a right fool, standing and pointing and beaming. I sat down. He didn't look up for a while, so we continued eating. We made some small talk, but it was obvious he was in a bad mood. I couldn't figure it out.

I thought about it later on my way home. The thought occurred to me that maybe, like Mark, he'd previously been involved in a failed pregnancy attempt. It was possible this kind of news stirred up memories of a miscarriage with a former partner.

Everyone had their own back story. Of course, I was sure that was it. His reaction had been completely the opposite of a normal reaction. Poor Ronnie, he'd make a super dad. He was so loving and caring and cuddly. And amazing with kids. Of course, I convinced myself that was it. Just like my female friends in their late thirties, he also heard that clock ticking and yearned to be a dad himself one day. I felt mean and selfish to gloat about my news to him. I needed to be more sensitive from now on. Poor Ronnie. I vowed to make it up to him somehow.

*   *   *

I barely saw Mark in the week that followed. All his time was taken up with work and securing the purchase of our new, dream family home. I started packing up stuff in the apartment and loading the car with charity bags. I'd prefer to do this stuff now while I was fit and capable, rather than wait until this bump got too big and heavy.

I spoke to the doctor about our plans to mind my mother in our new house and she thought it was a great idea because from my description, it was more wheelchair friendly than her own house with the steps out front. She required the address to pass on to the visiting physiotherapist and occupational therapist. She also wondered if there'd be periods when my mother would be home alone and suggested a key box out front, so the physicians could let themselves in while myself and Mark were at work. She also reassured me that my mother was already showing signs of gaining her strength back and was optimistic she'd be back on her feet in a matter of weeks.

I certainly hoped so, because I'd told Mark she'd only be with us for two weeks. When I saw her, I didn't think she'd be fit to go back to her own house after a fortnight. I enquired with the hospital social worker about getting a carer's package to support her when she eventually went home. I just wanted to be prepared. And ensure we wouldn't still be looking after her when our baby finally arrived. I showed Mark my research to reassure him that we wouldn't be stuck with her forever.

Over the next fortnight, my apartment went on the market and moving vans were booked for us to take what we wanted to our new home. It was so exciting. And incredibly exhausting. When we had the basics installed, we decided to spend our first night there. Mark cooked a warm, hearty Irish stew, got the TV working and we both slept like logs in the comfort of our new home. We were so happy, but didn't have time to bask. I was due to collect my mother from the hospital and Mark had plenty of odd jobs to do.

My mother smiled when she saw me arrive to take her home with me. She actually smiled! It warmed my heart and I knew I was doing the right thing. She wasn't overly effusive in her evaluation of our new house, but I got the impression she was impressed.

'I'm delighted we're so close to Bernadette,' she said. Her friend Bernadette lived only a short walk away in the next block of houses. I was glad of that too and looked forward to inviting her around. She'd already texted to welcome me to the neighbourhood.

* * *

The next day at work, Ronnie seemed to be avoiding me. I couldn't say for sure, but it seemed that way to me. I thought maybe we'd resume our lunch time get-togethers, but he slipped away for an early break and then spent the afternoon in the stock room clearing boxes. There was always loads to do in there, so he may have just been in the mood to get stuff done. Maybe he wasn't actually avoiding me and it was all in my head. I had no idea.

I found I was becoming absent-minded, more so than usual. The bigger my tummy grew, the more forgetful my brain became. I went for a walk after lunch to try to wake myself up. I stuck my headphones in and tuned in to talk radio. I listened to Julie Sinclair from time to time on *IrelandtalksFM*. She had interesting guests from around the country. On this particular occasion, she interviewed a guest about her midlife crisis that almost drew her to suicide. I was taken aback at her honesty, when she shared intimate details about her relationships and background. In the end, what saved her was a stint in therapy to address her dysfunctional background, introducing a daily yoga practice and listening to empowering meditations and self-help gurus.

It got me thinking about my own upbringing and I stopped in my tracks once or twice, wondering if mine was 'dysfunctional' too like the lady on the radio. I wondered if any of her strategies would help improve my life. I needed something to guide me through the fast pace of life changes I was going through at the moment—embarking on a serious relationship, becoming a first-time mother, selling my apartment, moving house and caring for my ailing mother. I was still attempting to hold down a full-time job through it all. And I was exhausted. As I made my way back to the library, I decided to visit the self-help section.

I found a variety of material that spoke volumes to me, like *Be the Person You Were Meant to Be*, *Connect with Your Inner Core* and *Trust Your Gut*. These were interesting titles to me and I made note of the ones that struck me. I didn't want to withdraw a ton of books since I was moving house, so I just borrowed one. The one that grabbed me the most. It was called *Heal and Reparent Your Inner Child*. I flicked through it and read the blurb—'*If only I had known this sooner, maybe my life could have been different.*' Hmmm, I was quite fascinated and wondered what it was that the author should have known. Would I know it? It also alluded to themes like shame and guilt, so I deemed it a suitable read for me. Time would tell.

When I got home that evening, Mark had helped my mother onto the couch. She was engrossed in the news, but managed a halfhearted nod as an acknowledgement that I was home. I didn't mind. I wasn't in the mood to chat. I was starving and tired, so I raided the fridge to satisfy my cravings. Mark came downstairs. He'd been on to the estate agent. An offer came through for my apartment, exceeding both our expectations and high above the asking price. We were ecstatic and accepted it straight away.

'This is it, Emma,' Mark smiled. 'This is the beginning of the rest of our lives.'

At that precise moment, the doorbell rang. It was the man with the van here to deliver my mother's bed. I'd ordered an orthopaedic bed based on advice from the physio. I knew she was only going to be staying for a couple of weeks, but I thought a nice, comfortable bed would be handy to have in the spare room and who knew, maybe eventually it would turn into a bed for our new baby once they'd outgrown their cot. I'd also remembered to take the support rail from her own bed the last time I dropped over to her house. She certainly came with a lot of paraphernalia, but she needed all the supports in her current condition. We set up the bed in the sitting room as she wouldn't be able to climb the stairs until her joints loosened up a bit. A few weeks of TLC and rigorous physiotherapy would see her right. At least, that's what I told Mark. And I told myself too, rather convincingly.

Chapter Seventeen

The *Heal and Reparent Your Inner Child* book came with a guided journal. Of course, I couldn't write in the one I'd borrowed from the library, but I Googled to find out where I could get my hands on a copy. It turned out it was available in a book shop called *Word Haven* on the MacMillan Road, near Dr Seán Dempsey's surgery where my pregnancy had been confirmed. I drove there after my shift at the library. I held it to my chest after purchasing it, like I knew it was meant for me or something. I bumped into Dr Seán on my way out of the shop. He stood back like a perfect gentleman and smiled to allow me pass, but there was no sign of recognition. He obviously had no recollection that he'd imparted to me the most important piece of information of my life only a few months previously. I guess I had a pretty forgettable face. Why would he recognise me anyway? I only recognised him because he was my doctor for a very brief but critical appointment. And he was memorable because he was extremely good-looking. Exceptionally so, I concluded, as I looked back to smile and bow to him in gratitude. He probably got that kind of attention from all his female patients, I imagined. Or maybe more... Who knew?

My mother was becoming increasingly demanding. She wanted the TV turned up very loud, claiming she couldn't hear it at our chosen volume level. She wouldn't drink the low-fat milk we bought and sent Mark out especially to buy calcium-enriched super milk for her bones. She also wanted early nights, which meant we had to tiptoe around the kitchen from nine pm every night because she was in the next room, and a light sleeper. Of course, the TV was wall mounted in the living room where she slept, so we missed our cosy nights zoning out on the couch watching old reruns of *Ally McBeal*. In Mark's words, 'she was really cramping our style' and I had to agree.

I arranged a half day midway through her second week with us, because I wanted to speak to the physiotherapist, who was due to call at two pm. My mother got a shock when I turned the key at 1.45. She wasn't expecting me. I'd actually forgotten to mention the half day. The living room door was open and she leaned back to check who it was.

'What's this? Checking up on me, are you?' she accused me before I had a chance to take off my coat.

'No, the physio's coming at two and I wanted to ask about your progress,' I clarified.

Her face fell. 'No, he's not. I rang to cancel him.'

'You what? I thought it was a 'her'—Jane something or other.'

'No, this isn't her area. She's based in Fairview. Thomas comes here to Malahide.'

'Thomas? I haven't met him,' I replied.

'Well, you won't meet him, will you?'

'Why not? Why did you cancel?'

'He's rubbish. And I didn't like his manner. He was a bit rude to me when I told him I was too tired for exercises.'

'But they only come twice a week. It's invaluable to your recovery and…'

'Look, if I'm not in the mood, I'm not in the mood, alright? They should respect that and come at a time when I'm feeling more energetic.'

'Mother! They're busy people travelling all over Dublin to see patients. They're on a schedule. We have to suit them, not the other way around!'

'Oh, you're as bad as he is,' she said and looked away.

I rang the hospital and asked if they could send someone else out. There would be no one available in the vicinity until five pm they informed me. Great! What a waste of a half day, I thought. I asked if there were any exercises I could do with my mother to strengthen her legs and joints in the meantime. They sent a link to a YouTube clip for recovering hip replacement patients. We watched it together and I tried to get her up with me to join in.

At this stage, she should be able to stand up unassisted, but she was still struggling and asking me for help. I did some of the basic exercises with her that she should be well able for, but she insisted she was getting tired and only attempted a few in a half-hearted fashion.

Doesn't she want to get better, I wondered. Why wasn't she trying harder? It wasn't like she was enjoying imposing on us, when we were so busy trying to settle into the house, hold down our jobs and attend hospital appointments now that the due date was getting closer. Or was she? Was she enjoying the knowledge that she was putting us out and inadvertently spoiling what should be a romantic time together making a home out of our new house? Was she? I knew what Mark would say. He was really getting to know her well. And it seemed the more he knew, the less he liked.

He definitely wasn't as patient as me with her. I saw him walk away exasperated on numerous occasions, trying to stop himself having it out with her. It seemed nothing he did for her was good enough. The handrail on her bedside was fixed too loosely and every time he tightened it, she claimed he made it worse. He overdid her toast and under-boiled her eggs. He made weak tea too, she said, so he gave up offering her a cuppa. He couldn't believe how ungrateful she was. He brought it to my attention that she never said thanks.

I looked at him wide-eyed, like why would she ever thank ME? That wasn't how she operated at all. But it got me thinking.

Why didn't she ever thank me? I was a good daughter. I did a lot for her. I sacrificed many nights out and weekends away to look after her over the years. And now, in my last trimester of my first pregnancy, I sacrificed settling into my new home in order to care for her when she needed me. But no. She never said thank you, Or asked me how I was. I choked a little when that thought popped into my brain. I thought of Patricia and the fuss she would be making of me now with my expanding bump. She'd be buying maternity blouses for me, knitting me baby blankets in anticipation and oohing and aaahhing over the scan photos. We'd be on this exciting journey of mine together. Patricia would have been a wonderful support to me. I was sure of that and I still missed her every day.

My mother didn't make that much of my pregnancy. She shared the news with her friends. I knew because some of them rang to congratulate me, but she didn't share any of her excitement or pride with me and I wasn't entirely sure if she felt any of those emotions. I didn't really know how she felt about it. All I detected was an air of dismissiveness, like it was nothing special and we've all done it and gotten through it and I should too, without any complaints. In fairness that's what

I did. I had no free time to dwell and wallow in pregnancy bliss. Every once in a while, Mark admired my bump and that was nice.

*   *   *

Two weeks later, and after I got a new physiotherapist organised for my mother, we noticed she started making more progress. She was beginning to push herself up from the armchair and stand by herself, unaided. This was progress. She also started walking around the sitting room with the support of a walking stick. Finally, she was following the physio's advice and Mark and I began to get excited that maybe she would be fit enough to return to her own home in a matter of weeks. The main aim for us was that she wouldn't still be in the house with us once our baby was born.

The cot, buggy and Moses basket were safely stored upstairs in the spare room, but we were hoping to add more baby paraphernalia to the living room once we cleared out my mother's single bed. It really took up a huge amount of space that we desperately needed in anticipation of our pending arrival.

Mark was starting to look up physio advice online, as my mother's next challenge now that she was walking around would be to manage walking upstairs and downstairs. He was helping her up the first three steps of our stairs and down. It was quite repetitive and draining, but he tried to stay positive amidst her barrage of complaints.

'You're moving too fast' or 'You're squeezing my arm' or 'You're getting in my way, I can do it by myself.' She wasn't exactly grateful for his help and encouragement, but he was a man with a plan and he wanted to send her packing back to her own home. I was caught in the middle to a certain extent. I was the one getting all the calls from her doctor, having to get her medication and facilitate house calls from medical professionals. On one occasion, when the occupational therapist got stuck in traffic and arrived late, I almost missed one of my antenatal appointments. That's how all-consuming my mother's follow-up medical treatment was.

With the welcome news that my brother and his partner were returning home for a holiday, respite was in sight. Alan was thankful that I'd taken care of our mother up to now and he offered to bring her home, back to her own house to look after her there. I enthusiastically accepted, thinking this would aid her transition to returning to independent living. Alan said he'd move her bed downstairs, so there'd be no rush for her to gain proficiency climbing stairs. She'd only need to manage the few steps up to the porch at the front door and of course, she wouldn't be alone attempting those. Himself and Sophie would help her settle in and we all hoped that at the end of their holiday, she could stay in her own home.

I, of course, hoped as much as anyone that this would be the case, but doubted my mother would agree. I felt she'd continue to demand my services and I'd be driving back and forth to her place every other day. That's why I liaised with the social worker at the hospital and we arranged a care package to kick in as soon as Alan left for the UK. She would be getting a morning carer to help her out of bed, get showered and ready for the day. Then, a carer in the afternoon to prepare her lunch and finally a carer in the late evening to assist her into bed, if necessary. It would be a local company providing the care package and it was heavily subsidised by the state. It was part of a rehabilitation package for elderly residents who wanted to live independently following hip or knee replacements or some such surgeries.

The alternative would be to receive rehab in a step-down facility or rehab centre until deemed fit enough to return home and I knew my mother wouldn't accept that. 'I'm not an invalid yet,' she'd say and then she'd worm her way back into our new family home and we'd all have to live in the pretence that she was part of it.

It was becoming increasingly obvious to me now that she would never really be part of our little family. She'd be a duty of care for us to oversee. I would forever concern myself with her overall wellbeing and safety, but as for her happiness, I was finally ready to unburden myself of that far-reaching goal. I'd be having a new little bundle of joy soon that would consume my desire to make someone happy. My new baby would win out hands down. I hoped my mother was ready to be pushed back in my list of priorities.

I hoped with every fibre of my being that I could finally focus on this new and exciting chapter of my life. I laid my hands on my tummy, sang to my bump and endlessly researched baby names and their meanings. Now that my mother had left our house, I started the nesting process of tidying, rearranging, painting and purchasing. I was feeling energetic and healthy and at each antenatal appointment I was informed of a strong heartbeat and the perfectly average weight and size of my unborn child. I felt free, optimistic and hugely hopeful for possibly the first time in my entire life.

Chapter Eighteen

At close to two weeks before my due date, I signed off on maternity leave at the library. Along with Ronnie, I interviewed a replacement librarian to take over my duties while I went on leave. We interviewed five prospective employees in total, four female and one male, all with varying qualifications and experience. However, we both knew instantly and intuitively who we'd choose when candidate number five came in. She was bright, bubbly and full of enthusiasm and I think we realised immediately how much the toddlers would love her. Our ultimate criteria in choosing my replacement was picking who would get on best with Patricia if she were still around. We knew straight away that Carol with her wide lovely eyes and engaging smile would be right up Patricia's street. At least myself and Ronnie were on the same page. I trained Carol over the course of my final week at the library.

It was getting close now. Only two weeks to go. Alan and Sophie returned to the UK and the care package kicked in for my mother. Of course she complained to no end that the morning carer was tardy and loud, the afternoon carer was a useless cook and the night carer was hard of hearing, so they couldn't communicate. However, when I visited the house myself after work on my last Friday shift at the library, I found it to be in a spotless condition. My mother was well fed, clean and fresh looking, so that told me she was being well looked after. Her fridge was fully stocked and I met the evening carer who was kind and softly spoken with an accent. It took a little getting used to, but I found after chatting for a few minutes I could understand her perfectly. I had a quiet word with my mother to be patient and give her a chance. What I really meant was, 'PLEASE BE NICE TO HER SO SHE DOESN'T QUIT, BECAUSE I'M NOT PREPARED TO CALL OVER EVERY NIGHT OF THE WEEK TO PUT YOU TO BED', but I phrased it in a slightly more subtle manner than that.

I returned home that evening to Mark and realised I had the next two weeks off to do nothing but rest and nest and prepare for our baby. Mark had an exhaustive list of plans to fill the time, but all I wanted to do was kick back and breathe a little. I wanted to take it in, the fact that I was going to become a mother. I had six books on motherhood borrowed from the library and I planned to read them all cover to cover.

Mark was hyper and fussy over the weekend. His parents came to visit and their excitement exhausted me, although I was grateful for their good wishes and advice. I had early nights and when Monday came, Mark went to work as usual and I smugly found myself alone at the kitchen table sipping my morning tea. Alone with my baby bump. Just me and my bump. I smiled to myself and felt an overwhelming sense of peace. I remembered something I'd read in my *Heal and Reparent Your Inner Child* journal, where the request was to write a letter to your unborn self to convey what it will mean to the world to have you in it. I decided to write a letter to my unborn baby instead, something I was fairly certain my own mother never did for me. I wanted to let my baby know that things would be different for them, unlike my own upbringing.

'Dear Baby,

I Love you. I Cherish you. I Want you.

I can't wait to meet you. I won't know what to do with you, so you'll have to help me. Guide me. Let me know what it is you want and more importantly, what it is you don't want. We'll journey together and find our way. Your daddy will help. He's so excited to meet you too. And your grandparents—they will dote on you. Well, I'm not too sure about your Grandma Angela, it's hard to say how she will react, but two out of three ain't bad.

I Love you. I Cherish you. I Want you.

I don't have all the answers. You should know that from the start. I'm learning every day. I'm lucky I work in the library, so knowledge is at my fingertips. We'll muddle through life together and read every day, so we can learn all we need to know. I'm going to start from scratch and do things differently to how I was raised. Maybe even the opposite. Whatever I need to do to ensure you feel loved unconditionally, because you are. And I haven't even met you yet! Whatever happens, whatever comes to pass in our future together, please know this and believe these words—

I Love you. I Cherish you. I Want you.

Love, hugs, kisses and cuddles,

Your Mom, Emma.'

Then I stayed at the kitchen table for another half hour and cried. I didn't know if it was the letter, the hormones or my expectations of what motherhood would involve, but I let it all out and was an emotional wreck all morning. On my first day off, alone in our new house, I bawled my heart out, but it felt somehow cathartic. It was time to confront my emotions, those I had suppressed due to not having the time to really feel them. Or the confidence to let them out. It felt right, and a sense of peace swept over me that afternoon. A knowing feeling that I was ready for what was coming my way. Ready to meet my new baby.

After a shower, my energy levels picked up and I cleaned, dusted, polished and scrubbed every inch of what was going to be the baby's nursery. I took breaks so as not to exert myself and around 4.30pm, I lay down on the couch to rest and daydream. My phone beeped. The interruption annoyed me at first, but when I saw Ronnie's name, I brightened up.

Ronnie
I hope you enjoyed your first day of freedom! I missed you here at the library, but Carol is getting on great so far. Here's something I've been working on for Friday..

I listened to the attached voice recording and it was Ronnie singing 'Miss Polly had a Dolly', followed by 'Little Bo Peep'. He had a knack for making songs out of nursery rhymes that were usually spoken, not sung. He had a soft, tuneful singing voice and in my mind, I could see him smiling as he sang. It made me smile too. My baby started to dance around in my tummy, so I played it again and held the phone to my bump. He or she was bopping away and it made me laugh. Then the quick rise and fall of my mountainous bump as I chuckled made me laugh even more. It looked hilarious and I couldn't stop myself. When I eventually came to, I replied to Ronnie.

Emma
That gets a thumbs up from me and a thumbs up from Bump! Now, get back to work! Don't you have another ten minutes of librarying to do?

Ronnie
Oooh, you've changed..

Then I sent back a smiley emoji.

When Mark came home, we had dinner together and he told me about his day. He stopped midway through a sentence and I raised my eyebrows.

'What?' I asked.

'Emma, did you even hear a word I just said?' he asked.

'Hmmm? Yes, yes, I was listening!' I insisted, although I couldn't recall anything he'd just said.

He laughed. 'You're so distracted. You're away with the fairies in another land. I guess this must be "baby brain" settling in?'

I laughed too. He was right. I had other things on my mind. I went to bed early, proud of what I'd achieved on my first day of maternity leave. I switched off my lamp but couldn't settle. I reached for my phone and listened once again to Ronnie's melodies and soft, reassuring singing voice. It helped me feel at peace and I went on to sleep like a baby that Monday night.

*   *   *

The next day wasn't so fruitful. I got a phone call at nine am from my mother's morning carer. When she arrived, she found my mother had gotten herself out of bed and in her attempts to get dressed independently, she'd fallen trying to put on her trousers. The carer sounded worried and reassured me that an ambulance was on its way. She told me she was afraid to move her in case anything was broken. She wanted to wait for the paramedics. She told me my mother was calling for me from the floor and passed the phone to her ear. My mother was calling for me? FOR ME? Really?

'Emma! Emma! Are you coming to get me?' she whined.

'Mother, stay put. Don't move. Wait for the ambulance…'

'Emma, Emma,' she repeated.

'Yes Mother, don't worry, I'm on my way. Don't stress, it's going to be okay,' I said, not knowing what was actually going to happen. I realised my hand was shaking. The carer came back on the line. 'She didn't wait for me. I wasn't late, she wanted to get up by herself to…'

'I know. I know what she's like. Ring me back when the ambulance arrives. I want to know whether I should go there or straight to the hospital.'

I packed a bag with snacks and books. If we were going to A&E, who knew how long we'd have to wait. The paramedic called me after what seemed like one minute but was actually ten.

'Hi Emma, your mother's going to be okay. I'm concerned her wrist may be fractured. She can't bend it, so we're bringing her straight to A&E.'

'Oh, and what about her hip? She fell and broke her hip six weeks ago and…'

'Yes, I know. She was able to tell me that. She's fully conscious. To be honest'—he lowered his voice—'this will set her back. Whatever progress she's made up to now will have to be made again. From scratch.'

My heart dropped. I had to sit down. He continued.

'Can you meet us at the hospital? She's asking for you.'

'She is? I mean, yes. Yes, of course, I'll be there in 15 minutes. Thank you. Thanks for everything', but the line went dead before I finished my sentence.

* * *

'A six-hour wait? Are you serious, Emma?' Mark was livid that I was back at the hospital looking after my mother in my current condition.

'She has no one else, Mark. I can't just leave her alone. The triage bandaged her arm. They're pretty sure there's a fracture. She needs an x-ray, but they informed me we could be waiting until four o'clock to be seen by a doctor. It's just so busy.'

He groaned. 'Your mother is more trouble than… Look, what do you need? I can drop over to you on my lunch break…'

'No, it's okay. I brought a bagful of snacks and there's a vending machine. It's too far for you to go on your lunch break.' I looked towards my mother. 'We'll be fine,' I said and I told him I'd ring him later. We sat in silence side by side, looking straight ahead, waiting to be called. I offered her a chocolate chip brioche and she accepted with her good hand. I smiled her way, thinking, she asked for me. She wanted me. She needed me. She called my name in her hour of need. It made me feel important, like I made a difference to her life and she had just somehow acknowledged it. I smiled again to myself when I thought about it.

I passed the time reading my library book, snacking on raisins and checking on my mother. I got a cushion from the car to make her more comfortable and visited the bathroom every half hour to relieve my own needs. Eventually, we were called by the doctor and the wrist fracture was confirmed. They would keep her overnight for observation and maybe longer to ascertain what supports she would need following her hip injury. I was sent home. She was tired but managed a wave. I was tired too. It had been a long day. I wasn't in the mood to stay up with Mark. I went to bed after dinner. I couldn't sleep. I listened to Ronnie's recording. The whole thing was less than two minutes long, so I listened a few times. Then, I settled and fell asleep. I didn't hear Mark creeping in beside me. I slept in and when I awoke, he'd already left for work.

Chapter Nineteen

'No,' he said. 'No, she's not coming back to live with us. Our baby is due in a week. I don't care how poorly your mother is. She can go and fend for herself. God knows, she has enough money put away to live off in her old age. And what's more, she didn't even say thank you the last time she stayed with us. All her meals, luxury downstairs accommodation, every whim was met, and she never said thanks for any of it. I'm sorry, Emma, I know she's your mother, but I'm not having her living with us again. She pushed all my buttons and has been taking advantage of you for years. It's time we took a stance and just said NO!'

He was determined. I got the distinct impression he hated her. This confused me. My partner and possibly husband-to-be, not to mention father of my as yet unborn child, hated the woman who gave birth to me and raised me. I'm not sure why, but I felt the urge to defend her. I mean, she wasn't THAT bad.

'But she needs me now, Mark. She asked for me.'

'What do you mean?' He looked puzzled.

'At the house when the carer arrived, she asked for me. She called my name.'

'But of course she did. You're all she has.'

'No, she has Alan too and plenty of friends and neighbours, but she asked for me. She called MY name.'

'But she knows you're the only one who will come. The others are acquaintances, not friends. And Alan's in the UK. You're all she has, Emma. Face it. That's why she asked for you. No one else would come.'

'Stop! Stop saying that. She asked for me because she needs me. She knows I'm the only one who can look after her properly.'

'Emma, what's wrong with you? Are you flattered because she called for you in her hour of need? She's using you. She takes, takes, takes from you, but gives nothing back.'

'Mark! She raised me!'

We both went quiet for a while. I put my head down. It was sore. I wanted to lie down and take a nap. It was Mark. He was doing this to me. He was making me feel stressed. All I wanted to do was to be there for my ageing, frail, sick mother. I just wanted to take care of her, like she…like she took care of…I started to cry. Why couldn't I finish that sentence in my head? Why did my own thoughts make me cry? Mark reacted.

'No, Emma, that won't work with me. Don't turn on the waterworks now and pretend you just want to be there for your poor, sick mother. I've had it up to here with that woman and the way she treats you. And look at you. You're not prepared to do anything about it. You seem happy to be her lapdog and at her beck and call.'

'Mark! What's wrong with you? Can't you see that I'm upset?'

'Yes, and I think you're only turning it on so I'll agree to having her back here living with us, but I won't. She's not welcome.'

I'd never seen him like this. I sat back on the couch and closed my eyes. I took a deep breath and put my hands to my giant belly. I felt it rise and fall with my breath. This was our first serious disagreement. Our first fight, maybe. We hadn't been together long enough to have had many. The last year had been such a whirlwind. I sank deeper into the couch and rubbed my belly. I confronted a niggling thought from the back of my mind that was raising its ugly head. I hadn't wanted to go there, or maybe I just hadn't had time.

I hardly knew him.

Or I didn't know him well enough to spend the rest of my life with him. This past year, we met for the first time. He seemed to like me, so we dated. I guess I must have liked him too, because I slept with him and became his girlfriend. He was there for me when Patricia passed away. It was nice to have someone to come home to. It was comforting. I think if I'd been coming home to an empty apartment, I would have gotten depressed or something, but having Mark was a godsend. A distraction.

I also appreciated his support when my mother had her accident. I'm not sure if I would have coped alone. I suppose I would have had to move in with her, as an apartment wouldn't have been a suitable space for her to recover. But now we had a lovely, comfortable house, with no stairs for her to climb. We'd been able to make it safe for her by installing her bed downstairs in the living room. I didn't think I could have managed all of that on my own. But his support for her had expired now and all he wanted was his baby. Our baby. In fairness, he'd wanted that from the start.

It almost seemed like he wanted that more than he ever wanted me. He wanted a girlfriend who could conceive for him, a house in the suburbs and a family of his own. I started wondering if HE was using ME. Just like he accused my mother of doing. Was he doing the very same thing? Was he on the dating scene just to meet the mother of his child? And not to meet someone that he could potentially fall in love with?

When I opened my eyes, he was looking at me. Maybe he was wondering if he'd gone too far. I felt I needed to say something.

'I don't like you talking about her like that. Maybe I'll give out and complain about her taking advantage of me from time to time, but I don't think it's your place to belittle her.'

'I'm only doing it for you. So, you'll realise…' he snapped back.

'Let me come to my own conclusions,' I said, softly.

'Just don't make any rash decisions and invite her back here before our baby is born, okay? Don't let her talk you into anything. I don't care that she asked for you or called your name. This is our family house and I want to keep it like that. Just the three of us, okay?'

He'd made it abundantly clear that allowing my mother to recuperate here with us this time was not an option.

* * *

'What do you mean I can't come and stay? The cheek of him! I'm your mother, Emma! If you don't look after me now in my hour of need, who will? WHO WILL?'

'Look, we can increase the care package and…'

'The care package? It was with the care package that I sustained this injury. Sure, they're no good to me. No good at all.'

'Well, I won't be much good to you either in my current condition, will I? There's not much I can do for you…'

'And all the sacrifices I made for you over the years…'

'What?' I snapped. We both jumped. She looked wide-eyed.

'What's that supposed to mean?' she asked.

'What sacrifices are you talking about?' I asked in a softer tone. An almost despairing one. I just wondered, because I'd heard her speak of these sacrifices on many occasions, but she never elaborated on exactly what they were. It was always in general terms. I didn't know if she meant childbearing was a sacrifice for her, because she didn't want them. She never wanted children and maybe she only did it because that's what society and her husband expected of her. I genuinely wanted to know.

'Don't ask silly questions like that,' she said dismissively. 'You'll know all about the sacrifices when that baby of yours is born.'

I instinctively felt my tummy. He or she was kicking wildly. They must have sensed their mother was under attack. Again.

'That baby of mine, as you put it, is going to be your grandchild you know. Aren't you excited about becoming a granny for the first time?' I asked.

'I'm too old to be getting excited about such things.'

'Oh.' I looked down. I would have cried if I had the energy, but I didn't. I was wiped. I was miserable. And all at the hands of my supposed loved ones. My nearest and dearest. My mother and my partner. I thought of Patricia and how much I missed her. What a difference she'd made to my life for so many years. She'd been my rock when my mother had been at her most demanding. I could share everything with her and she'd listen. Sometimes she'd offer advice, but she knew when not to. She never tried to intervene when it came to my 'mother issues'. She understood it wasn't her place. She knew it was a sensitive subject for me and she had faith that I'd eventually come to my own conclusions.

Whilst driving home from the hospital, I thought of Ronnie. I didn't know why. Maybe I missed him or something. Or possibly thoughts of Patricia brought him to mind. I hadn't heard from him in a while. Not since he'd sent me the voice recording of the songs for the toddlers. It made me smile just thinking about it. I wondered how himself and Carol were coping with the Friday toddlers. I decided to phone him when I got home.

'Emma? Is that you?' He sounded surprised to hear from me.

'Hey! Yeah, how are you? I was wondering how the toddler mornings are going?'

'Oh, the toddler mornings, right, of course. Yeah, well, they're going really well in fact.'

'Oh excellent! I hoped so. Tell me more!' I insisted.

'Well, my songs went down a treat. Even the mums and dads were singing along and some made requests for their favourite nursery rhymes to be put to song!'

'Hah!' I laughed. 'You're taking requests now! That's hilarious!'

'Yes, only from the under-threes though. Keep it simple, you know. I don't want to have to go learning new chords or anything!' We both laughed and it reminded me of the fun we had working together. We had the exact same childish sense of humour. I didn't share that with anyone else. I realised I missed Ronnie.

'I miss you,' I blurted out. 'I mean, working with you. Like, I miss the library and…'

'It's not the same without you, Emma,' he replied, and his words did something to my heart. Made it all soft like jelly. I took a minute to respond.

'And Carol? She's working out? We made the right choice, right?' I needed reassurance that Patricia's wishes for the toddler mornings to flourish were being met.

'Yes, we did. She's great. She was going to apply for a primary teaching course, but she actually loves working in the library so much that she didn't even send in the application. She's putting it off until further down the line because she's having so much fun developing the children's activities in the library. It will be an experience that will stand to her if she decides to go ahead with the teaching and...'

'What?' I asked.

'Patricia would be proud.'

'Oh,' I said, as my heart swelled. We shared the same priorities. It all just made me want to cry, so I made excuses that there was someone at the door and I had to go and then I went to the couch to have a big, fat cry.

I was crying a lot lately, but at least these were happy tears that Patricia's hopes were being fulfilled at the library. I made a mental note to call her family and let them know how things were going. I lay back and drifted off to sleep on the couch. Mark woke me when he arrived home from work. He presented me with a bouquet of lilies. In fact, he pushed them so close to my face that I may have accidentally inhaled some of the orange pollen powder. Yuck, I thought. 'Thanks,' I said. He was beaming.

'Not long to go! Only five days until we get to meet our little creation!' he announced.

Our what? 'Oh, that's assuming I go on my due date. You know that rarely happens on the first baby. It's normal to go a few days over...'

'I'm so glad you said that!' he smiled.

'Said what?' I think I was still half asleep.

'On the first baby! I'd love to have more too!' he clarified.

Alarm bells triggered in every vein and nerve ending in my body. 'Oh no, no I didn't mean it like that. I just meant typically on the first baby, it's normal to go overdue by a few days. According to all the books I've read and what I've heard. I was speaking in general terms, I didn't mean...' I burped suddenly. Then I retched. And then I puked. All over the carpet in our new house.

Chapter Twenty

'Oh God,' I said. 'Look! Look what I've done.'

'Don't mind the carpet, Emma! It's the baby! This happens. It might be the onset of labour! Are you having contractions yet? Lie back, get comfy.'

'No! I'm not lying back. I've got vomit on my face! Will you get me a cloth?'

He dashed to the kitchen full of excitement, while I remained on the couch, full of bile. When he came back, I wiped my face and told him I was going to take a shower.

'Should we…should we prepare to go to the hospital, Emma?' he asked, with what I thought looked like a deranged expression in his eyes. It was probably just nerves mixed with excitement though.

'No. I don't think it's happening tonight. I just puked, that's all. I might go to bed after my shower, okay?' I handed him my dirty face cloth and turned towards the bathroom. When I got there, I locked the door and sat on the toilet seat to think. *Am I okay?* I just puked. *What does that mean? Is something wrong? Could something be wrong? Is that normal? To puke five days before your due date?* I felt okay. I felt my tummy. Yes, my baby was moving. Movement was good. I felt okay. I concluded there was no need to panic.

I showered and moisturised and put on my fluffiest, softest pyjamas before crawling into bed. I rubbed my bump tenderly and cuddled myself. I needed some comforting. I stroked my purple, fluffy pyjamas and felt them warm my skin. I gave myself comfort and realised I didn't want it from anyone else. I was enough for me tonight. I hoped I was enough for my baby too, for we both slept soundly for ten hours. Like babies in fact. The peace and the rest was urgently required. I didn't realise it then, but I had a major life decision pending and for the first time in my life, I was going to suit no one but myself.

* * *

Mark must have fallen asleep on the couch. His body was still imprinted in the fabric and the cushions were stacked like pillows. He entered as I was fixing it up.

'Good morning!' he sang.

'Hi, did you sleep here last night?' I asked.

'Yeah, well I fell asleep and eh, no offence, but your snoring woke me around one am. I got up and you were so deeply asleep that I didn't want to disturb you, so I slept in the spare room.'

'Oh no! I bet I was on my back, was I?'

'Yes!' He nodded.

'Sorry about that, Mark. Did you sleep okay in the other bed?'

'Sound, thanks.'

Hmmm, I thought, our baby wasn't even born yet and we were already in separate rooms. Wasn't that supposed to happen later, when the baby starts to keep us awake?

He opened the fridge. 'Rashers, sausages, eggs?' he asked.

'Oh God no. No way. Not after getting sick last night. I couldn't. I'll just have a bowl of cornflakes.'

'Emma, you need to keep your energy levels up. You could go into labour any second from now on, you know.'

'I just can't stomach that kind of fried food right now. You go ahead. I'll make tea.'

He heated the pan, added two sausages first, then two rashers and got the small egg frying pan. The oil was spitting a bit, so I handed him the splatter shield. As he took it from me he said, 'Emma, you know I was thinking, we should probably get married.'

'Excuse me! What did you say?' I wasn't sure if I'd heard him correctly. Was he thanking me for the splatter shield or asking me to marry him?

'You know, it makes more sense to be married for our kid, going forward.'

I smelled something burning. 'You need to flip those rashers,' I offered.

'Oh shit, yeah, thanks. So, em, what do you think? Like, how do you feel about it?' he asked, as he turned over the rashers and sausages on the pan.

'Me?' I didn't know how I felt. I hadn't had a chance to sit down yet and sip some tea. I was nine months pregnant and had just slept for ten hours. My baby had nibbled all my supplies. I needed some tea or milk or water or something before I could consider such a question.

'Do we have any kitchen paper?' Mark asked.

'Hmmm? Sorry?'

'I want to drain these. They're dripping. Where's the kitchen paper?' He really didn't want oily sausages on his plate and they needed to come off the pan.

'It's under the sink.'

'Thanks,' he said. I made a pot of tea and poured milk on my flakes. We sat down at the kitchen table to have breakfast.

'So, as I was saying,' Mark began, but then my phone frightened the life out of both of us. I answered immediately and was never so happy to hear my mother's dulcet tones. She was calling from the hospital with a list of requests. Relief swept through my body as she requested her Clarks slippers, 7 Up, a hand towel, a new dressing gown and a box of tissues. I got up to get a pen and paper. I wrote it all down, knowing I'd forget everything as soon as I put the phone down.

'I'll get all that straight away. See you in about an hour,' I said in my chirpiest, most grateful voice. I don't know if I ever felt such gratitude for my mother as I did right there and then, halfway through my cornflakes on a Saturday morning.

'I have to go as soon as I finish this, Mark. She's low on supplies at the hospital and…'

'But we were having a serious conversation about our relationship and what's best for our baby and…'

'No, we weren't. You were. I was eating my breakfast.'

He just looked at me blankly. I think I'd rendered him speechless. I didn't know I could do that, but it felt good and it felt right at this particular moment. I got up, put my bowl in the dishwasher and brought my mug of tea upstairs. I needed to get dressed and get ready for the day. But, more than anything, I needed not to be in the same room as Mark right now.

*   *   *

As I drove to my mother's house I couldn't escape my emotions. I felt low and deflated and for the first time in a long time, it wasn't at the hands of my mother. It was all because of Mark. I had that niggling feeling again. *He doesn't know me. He doesn't really know me.* And now, miraculously, we were about to have a baby together.

I pulled into my mother's driveway and stayed in the driver's seat. I undid the seatbelt so I could relax my belly and I put both hands on my bump. Everything that was happening right now would have consequences for my baby's future. Our baby's future. I rubbed my bump in firm, circular motions. I hoped it was soothing for the little person in there. I didn't want them to worry about any of this. I rested my head back and closed my eyes, while my hands moved around and around.

Big deep breath. Another one. He was talking about marriage for the sake of 'the kid'. Not marriage because he'd fallen madly, deeply in love with me. More deep breaths were urgently required.

I made myself face up to some facts. I didn't crave his company. I didn't crave his touch. In fact, I don't think I'd ever appreciated my own company and my own touch until I moved in with Mark. I spent more time trying to escape him than join him.

And now, today, my mother's demands proved to be a welcome distraction from him. I never thought that day would come. I was under the impression that my priorities were changing from my old family to my new family. From my mother to my partner, but now I realised HE was not going to be a priority for me. HE was the one I just gobbled up my cornflakes for, in order to execute a swift getaway from. And my mother was the one I was going towards. But only as an excuse. I opened my eyes and leaned forward. I looked down to my bump. *Here is my real priority. My one and only true priority. Along with myself.* If I didn't include myself, it wouldn't make sense. After all, we were in this together—literally! I would do what was right for me AND them. From here on, us two would be the only way forward. The two of us would find our path. 'We two' would strive for harmony and happiness together.

I got out of the car with a bounce in my step. In record time, I sourced whatever I needed from my mother's house. I drove to the shops and picked up a box of tissues and the most beautiful, expensive, softest dressing gown I could find. I picked one up for me too. I smiled and looked down. 'For us two,' I whispered to my bump and smiled. We were going to be just fine. This baby inside me was giving me strength and confidence, affording me power that I never knew I had. Every ounce of unused autonomy inside of me was going to be awakened for the first time in its life.

I was a half hour late getting to my mother's bedside, but I swanned in revealing the velvety texture of the luxurious animal print dressing gown.

'It's grotesque!' she exclaimed. 'I'm not wearing that! It looks like something Elvis Presley would have worn in his final drug-fuelled days. Put that back in the bag immediately!'

Another first for me—I didn't do as she ordered. I burst out laughing instead. I howled with laughter as my belly shook violently up and down, up and down. The other sick patients in the ward looked over quizzically, so I stuck my face in the soft fabric of the gown to muffle my guffaws. My mother looked wide-eyed until I managed to stop.

'You're right!' I said. 'It smacks of that era and I can just picture Elvis frolicking on his leopard print couch draped in a gown such as this! Hahahahaha.' I continued laughing. I couldn't help myself.

'What's gotten into you? Everyone's looking over. You're an embarrassment to me!' She looked cross. I didn't let it get to me. I pulled the full dressing gown out and pushed it towards her face. 'Look, feel this. Smell this. Isn't it just the best thing you've ever felt? I bought one for myself too. We should wear them together some time!' That idea just came to me, but from the look I was met with, I quickly realised that no, that was NEVER going to happen. Patricia would have LOVED a gift like this, I briefly thought.

I put the dressing gown back in my bag. I'd keep that one now that I'd mauled it and go back and return the other one. I showed her everything else I'd bought or collected and didn't get into trouble for anything else. It was just the dressing gown I was in the bad books for. Oddly, that fact made me smile. My mother didn't know what to make of me that Saturday morning and I delighted in her discombobulation.

'We two,' I muttered under my breath with one hand on my tummy and the other carrying the bag with my new dressing gown in it. As I left my mother and made my way to my car, I repeated 'we two' a few times and it gave me great comfort.

Chapter Twenty One

I didn't go straight home after the hospital. I drove by my old apartment instead. The 'Sale Agreed' sign stood tall and proud outside at the front gate. I felt a pang in my heart. I'd been happy there. Fully independent. I never had to hide in a room, away from someone else. It was just me. Yes, I felt lonely from time to time, but I always got over it by distracting myself with work, or meeting a friend, or pandering to my mother or talking to Patricia. I used to find something to snap me out of that lonely feeling.

But now, with this baby kicking and prodding in my tummy, I didn't expect I'd be feeling lonely any time soon. Me and them, 'we two', would keep each other company from now on. I drove home and a flutter of relief overcame me when I saw that Mark's car wasn't in the driveway.

I went straight to the kitchen and made scrambled eggs and toast. I sat down to devour it and noticed a text from Mark to say he'd just popped out to the shops to pick something up for dinner. I relaxed in my own company for a while. Then, I went to the drawer and found a pen and some scrap paper. I decided to carry out a task I'd seen and ignored in my *Heal and Reparent Your Inner Child* journal. I knew it was upstairs in my bedside locker, but I also knew Mark would be home any minute and I didn't have much time. The energy to leg it upstairs and get it escaped me, so I unlocked my memory to picture the layout of the page. I proceeded to divide my page into two columns and wrote the headings 'Working' and 'Could Be Better'. I made a list of everything in my life that I considered to be working well for me, like my health, my income, my job, my pregnancy, my appetite and my friend Ronnie.

Then, I listed the areas in my life which had room for improvement, like my relationship with Mark, my relationship with my mother, my mental health and my lack of real, meaningful friends now that Patricia had passed away. It seemed Helen and Julie had dropped me because I'd met someone and gotten pregnant before them. We all thought I'd be the last to reach those milestones because I tried the least out of the three of us. I guess there were feelings of bitterness at their ends but it only made me feel that we never really had a proper, honest connection in the first place. If they weren't happy for me now, then maybe we were never real friends to begin with. I didn't seem to miss them that much anyway. I didn't have time.

The next heading I remembered from my journal was 'A Year From Now'. I wrote it down on the back of my piece of scrap paper. Hmmm. I had to think. A year from now. Where would I like to be? Who would I like to be? Who would I like to be with? What would I be doing? I tapped the pen a few times on the kitchen table to buy some thinking time. Hmmm. I heard Mark pulling into the driveway. By the time he unloaded shopping from the boot, I reckoned I had about two minutes to write something down. So, I wrote the first thing that came into my mind—'Right here, with my baby.'

I folded the piece of paper and tucked it in my pocket. I'd read it again tonight and maybe make a few additions. I got up and threw the pen back in the drawer. As I turned around, Mark was standing there with a bunch of roses and a big grin on his face. He shoved them towards me.

'Ow,' I said as I pricked my finger on a thorn. 'I mean, thanks, they're beautiful.' And they were. Scarlet red roses bunched together with a sheer organza red ribbon. So beautiful. But I didn't want them. I didn't want them from Mark. My heart sank. I knew at that moment that if I didn't want to accept these roses from him, then there was nothing he could ever do to make me happy. I looked at him and he got down on one knee.

'Emma,' he said.

'No,' I said. 'Mark, get up!'

'But you don't understand, I was going to ask…'

'Ahhh!' I squealed, putting my hand to my forehead like a damsel in distress. In fairness, I was in distress.

'Emma! Are you okay? Is it the baby?' he yelled.

I took the time to look him in the eye. He just wanted a baby. He didn't really care so much about me. He was looking for a vessel to carry his offspring and I willingly provided him with that. But now, the tables had turned and that was just what I wanted too, a baby. It was all I wanted—our baby, my baby. I didn't want him any more than he wanted me. I didn't really need him either, although I conceded he needed me desperately. After all, I was carrying his child.

'Will I ring the hospital, Emma? Are you having contrac…?'

I reached my hand out in a stop sign. 'No, no. Just let me sit down please.' He took the roses from me and pulled out a chair. 'Ouch,' he said. I guessed the roses pricked him too. I sat down.

'What's wrong?' he asked.

'Mark, I think we should break up.'

Silence.

He paced around the kitchen. He walked in circles. It made me feel dizzy. I put my head down.

'Emma, what's gotten into you? You're acting very strange. Is it your hormones?' he asked, rubbing his chin, as though I were a problem to solve.

'Em, I don't know. I'm sure I am quite hormonal with only days to go, but…' I looked up and he was staring at me. So, I continued. 'This is what I want. I don't love you. I'm not in love with you. I'm in love with our baby and I want to thank you for having a baby with me. And I want you to be our baby's daddy. I know you'll make a wonderful father, but I don't want to be in a relationship with you. I'm sorry.'

'My mother was right about you,' he said.

'What? What do you mean?' I was confused.

'She said if a person's relationship with their mother is as dysfunctional as yours, then you're dealing with a damaged person. And you're damaged, Emma. You can't see it, but she's ruined you and you'll never be happy. If you're trying to leave me now, you'll never find anyone to make you happy. This is your loss if you go through with this. YOUR loss!' He pointed my way with anger in his eyes. I took in his words for a few moments before responding. I stood up.

'That's not true,' I said, as I stood up. 'I've already found someone who makes me happy.' I gestured to my bump with tears in my eyes. 'I've got someone inside me who makes me happy.'

'Don't you dare try to take my baby away from me! Don't you threaten me!'

I held out my hand, horizontally, palm down. 'Mark, you don't understand. I'm not trying to take your baby away from you. It's our baby and I want to have it with you. I just don't want to be your wife, that's all.'

'But what about this?' he shouted. 'What about all this that we created together for our family?' He swung his arms wide around the kitchen.

'Yes, yes, I know. I love our house and I love what we've made of it,' I said softly. Then, I paused and waited for his eyes to meet mine. I insisted on eye contact for what I was about to say. 'Face it Mark, I don't love you and YOU don't love me. Be honest with me. You know I'm right.'

He left the room, slammed the front door and I heard his car drive away. I remained on the chair for a few minutes to catch my breath and rub my tummy. I'd never stood up to anyone like this before. I'd never had the courage to be honest about my own needs or my own feelings. I looked down and gave full credit to the little being inside me. They were giving me strength, courage and confidence. I was doing this for both of us. Maybe I just never had anyone that I loved so completely to stand up for before and that was spurring me on. I guess I'd undervalued my own requirements up to now, because it was just me. Just obliging, obedient Emma Ward, eager to please.

I felt strength rise within me, coming from my tummy. I felt it in my gut. In my heart. I felt for the first time in my life I was being true to myself, acknowledging my inner feelings that I'd dismissed for so long. I thought about what Mark said. There was truth in it. My mother treated me like a second class citizen and I believed I was. But that cycle of belief would change, as of now. I took the piece of scrap paper from my pocket and marched upstairs to get my journal. I copied everything I'd written and proceeded to write more. I wrote a plan. I used the spare 'Notes' pages at the back of the journal and filled it with possibilities of how my future would look and added steps I would need to take to make it happen.

'Damn!' I exclaimed when I'd reached the last page. 'Damn it!' I repeated, as I read through what I'd written. There was no denying it. My mother featured heavily in every eventuality I'd concocted for my future and that of my baby's.

Chapter Twenty Two

Mark didn't come home that night. He texted to say he was staying over with his parents to process what I'd told him. He said to call if I felt contractions or needed to go to the hospital. I thanked him and told him I felt just fine and wasn't experiencing any flutters. He said he'd come over in the morning to talk things through.

I slept like a baby. I woke up refreshed and rejuvenated, like a new woman. The hospital rang. They wanted to meet me to discuss my mother's progress. I genuinely hoped they weren't going to put pressure on me to take her home. Surely, they'd see that I was about to give birth any day and wouldn't be a fit carer for her. And if they didn't, surely I'd have the sense to refuse and share with them that I am now a single parent going forward. I straightened my shoulders and puffed out my chest when I thought about that. I'd have to get used to acting strong and confident for my baby. And, for me...

When I walked into the ward, my mother looked up expectantly.

'Are you here to take me home?' she asked. 'I hate the food. I got burnt sausages for breakfast this morning…'

'Hi, no, I'm here to meet the doctors to discuss…'

'I want to go home, Emma. You tell them not to keep me here any longer.'

'But you can't walk. You need intensive physio. I can't take you anywhere if you can't walk!'

'Rubbish! I was well able to get around the ground floor of your house and…'

'But you could walk then, with a crutch. You can't even stand up now. I'm sorry to say, but you're going to be wheelchair bound for the foreseeable future until you get strong enough to walk again.'

'I'll get up. I always do. I'll get back up!'

'I've no doubt you will, but it's going to take time and until then, I can't take you anywhere. Look at me!' I pointed to my tummy, trying to get her to see me, really see me, but she sighed and looked away, exasperated. That's when the doctor approached.

'Emma, thank you for coming. I can only imagine how difficult it is to come into the hospital when it's not an antenatal appointment. You must be sick of this place!'

'Oh no, that's okay. I think it will be more difficult when Baby arrives. Better now than then!'

She laughed. 'Yes, very true! And how are you feeling?'

'Excuse me?' It just came out. I really wasn't used to being asked that question. 'Oh, me? I'm feeling, well, I guess I'm feeling okay. I'm not sure, though.' What a lame answer, but I hadn't thought about how I felt yet that day. I'd just gotten up, dressed and came straight to the hospital.

'You look well, not long to go! Would you like to follow me to the meeting room?' she offered.

I looked back at my mother. She looked so sad. She pulled the covers up and tucked herself in. 'I won't be long,' I said, trying to sound reassuring. She looked away, like an abandoned puppy.

The doctor told me the honest truth—they needed the hospital bed. My mother was eligible to be transferred to a rehabilitation centre, where she would receive intensive physio for approximately three weeks. Following that, she would be assessed to ascertain whether she would be fit to return home or be referred for 24-hour care. It would all depend on how the rehab went. It made perfect sense to me and I hoped she would make the necessary progress to return to independent living. Unfortunately, I was the one who had to break the news to her. I approached her bedside following the meeting with very low expectations.

'You're sending me where?' she roared.

'No, no, listen, I'm not "sending" you anywhere. The doctor prescribed a rehab facility for you to recover and learn to walk again. Then…'

'You're getting rid of me, aren't you? I knew you would. You and Alan, you're in cahoots, I know you are!' she accused, as was her wont.

'No, no, Mother, listen! If you go to rehab for three weeks, they will assess you then, and if they think you're fit to go home, they'll send you home and you can live independently like you used to and get back to all your…'

'I want a second opinion!' she demanded.

I paused. Baby was kicking like a cage fighter. Ouch! I was getting tired and needed to go and eat. 'Well, I'm not sure why you feel the need to go for a second opinion. I have full confidence in the doctor I spoke to at the meeting and you must agree to some extent. I mean, you can't walk unaided. Actually, at the moment, you can't walk at all, because you can't put pressure on your wrist to use the crutch. You're completely wheelchair bound until your wrist heals. Of course, you need this step-down facility. There's NO OTHER OPTION!'

She looked at me wide-eyed. She hadn't been expecting me to rant, but it was true. Everything I said was true and there was no getting away from it. I didn't give her a chance to contradict me.

'I'm starving! I have to go. NOW!' I pointed to my belly and walked away. I knew I was leaving her full of questions, but this baby inside me was demanding to be fed. They had gnawed through my insides and were content to leave me weak, but I couldn't take it. It was do or die, so I left without a backward glance. I knew I had to prioritise. I had to look after ME and my baby, and that's what I did.

*   *   *

When I got home, Mark called. 'Can I come over?' he asked.

Munching on breadsticks, I managed, 'If you bring hot food.' I didn't feel like cooking. When I finished four dry breadsticks, I started nibbling on raisins and chopped apple. It was helping but it wasn't enough. Relief swept through me when Mark walked through the door twenty minutes later with a single of chips. 'Bliss!' I exclaimed, covering them in salt and vinegar. He hovered around the kitchen while I stuffed my face. Eventually, he spoke.

'My mother wanted me to apologise for what I said, you know, about you being damaged. She's mortified I told you that.'

'Oh, okay. Well, tell her not to worry. I was thinking about it too. Maybe there's some truth in that. I've been journaling lately and it's helping me to figure things out.'

'What do you mean?' he asked.

'Well, I know that my mother is a toxic person and usually the advice regarding toxic people is to walk away and remove them from your life. But when it's your own mother, it's different. I can't just...' I trailed off and got up to get some water.

'You could stand up to her, Emma. You seem to just let her walk all over you. I'm doing you a favour by calling it out.'

'I'm getting to the point where I feel confident enough to stand up to her, but I've felt that you were rushing me and pressuring me. You wanted me to stand up to her for the wrong reasons.'

'I don't understand. What are you trying to say?'

'You wanted me to stand up to her, for YOU, not for ME. It was to remove the headache of her from your life, not to make things better for me. I'm nearly forty years old and I've lived with this relationship with my mother all my life. You were so clinical about it. I can't just become estranged from her because she's putting you out. This is a huge decision that I have to make, myself, for me. And now I guess every decision I make is for our baby too. I have to be careful and do the right thing.'

'And do you think the right thing is breaking up with me? Is that the right thing for our baby going forward?'

I sipped more water. I'd added way too much salt to those obviously already salted chips. What was I thinking?

'I don't know, Mark. It just seemed to hit me all of a sudden that we're not in love with each other. We fell in with each other because we both desperately wanted to meet someone. I guess we were at that stage of our lives when our peers were settling down and we didn't want to get left behind. It was great at the start. Honestly, I was so happy. You were everything I was looking for. But then things moved way too quickly in such a short space of time and our relationship suffered.'

'We can get back to that, Emma. Back to how it was at the start. I've a bunch of flowers in the car. I didn't know whether to bring them in.'

'No. No, don't. I don't want them. Give them to your mother. Tell her they're from me as a token that I forgive and understand what she said about me and why she said it.'

He stood there with a blank stare in his eyes. I carried on.

'Mark, I'm at the stage in my life where I feel strong enough to take control of my relationships. I think our baby is giving me strength and I think I'm doing this for them. I know, deep in my heart, that right now I don't want to marry you. I don't want to continue a romantic relationship with you either. I need time by myself to figure things out.'

He looked forlorn. I continued.

'Look, maybe at some stage in the future, our relationship will reignite, but for now, I want us to focus on being the best parents for our little one that we can be. Our baby is going to be lucky. They will have a devoted mother and father and I know your parents will dote on them too. They will have four people rooting for them, loving them and cherishing them. That's so much more than I ever had. I hadn't much of a relationship with my father because he was distant and non-communicative. My mother had narcissistic tendencies, so the maternal spirit never lived in her or she shut it out or something. The only functional relationship I grew up with was the one with my little brother, but he always had other stuff going on and friends or girlfriends that he'd rather spend time with. Our baby will be cherished by four adults and I'm focussing on that and how much they will be loved by all of us. We don't need to force a relationship for them. We need to be honest and compassionate and respect each other.'

He sighed. 'Wow, I wasn't expecting that! That journaling has really informed you. I've never heard you speak with such clarity.' Oooh, that gave me a warm, fuzzy feeling and confirmed that I was on the right track in my own personal journey. He continued. 'I need to process all of that, but I want to be here when our baby arrives. I can park our relationship troubles for now, but I want to soak up every breath of our baby's life from the very beginning. Emma, I'm not staying with my parents again. I'll take the spare room and make it my own for now, until we work things out.'

'Ewww,' I said. 'Those chips. I think I ate them too quickly.' Massive wave of pain. 'Ahhhh,' I howled.

'Here, come on, lie down on the couch. You did wolf them down. I noticed that. And all that salt... I'll go get a bucket in case you barf again.' He turned to go but I called him back.

'Ahhh,' I screamed as another wave of pain pulsated through my abdomen. 'Don't do that. Get the car keys! Ahhh! Mark, I think it's happening! And soon! Ahhh!'

Chapter Twenty Three

Niamh Ward Mooney was born that day about three hours later in the maternity wing of the same hospital my mother was in. I cried when she was presented to me swaddled in the blue hospital blanket. I cried with the knowledge that my own mother was in the same building and wasn't sharing this special moment with me. I cried because I knew deep down that Niamh would be raised by parents who weren't united in a steady relationship. But most of all I cried with wonder at how beautiful she was, and how much I loved her already and how determined I was to do everything differently to what I imagined my mother did with me. I guess in reality I cried too because I'd just given birth and it was an enormously emotional experience. I was pretty certain most women cry after giving birth. I remembered reading it in one of my pregnancy books.

Mark cried too. I'd never seen him so happy. He was on the phone already to both his parents sharing his joy. I experienced a slight pang of jealousy. I had no one to share my joy with. If Patricia were alive, I probably would have rung her or texted. I knew I'd let Alan and Sophie know first, and then I supposed my colleagues in the library would be informed next.

Mark was mesmerised by Niamh. He'd wanted a baby so badly and he was beyond himself with excitement. I noted he didn't look me in the eye once since Niamh was born. I was secondary. His behaviour served to confirm my belief that he didn't really love me at all. He'd gotten what he wanted from me, but I twisted it as much as I could into a positive scenario, as I knew he'd make a wonderful dad and Niamh would be loved so much by both of us.

I stayed in the hospital learning how to bond with and how to breastfeed my baby girl. I was emotional and exhausted, riding high when she latched on and screaming in pain when she didn't. It was toe curling and excruciating, but I, or we, eventually got the hang of it and we were deemed ready for discharge. For all and sundry it seemed as though myself and Mark were a loving couple and I suppose we were, but all our love was directed towards Niamh.

He drove us home and the next few weeks were filled with love, baby cuddles and anxiety about whether she got enough breastmilk or too much. We questioned her weight, her complexion, her breathing and her movements. I was fluctuating between extreme highs to baby blues and back up again. Mark's parents were wonderful, insisting I go and get some rest while they watched Niamh. Mark returned to work after ten days. His parents offered to visit when it was just me and Niamh, but under the circumstances, I preferred if they just came when Mark was home. Besides, I needed to get used to mothering on my own.

And I did. We fell into a routine of feeding and resting and stretching out the sleep cycles until she was able to go down for six or seven hours without waking. When she was two months old, I brought her into the library to show her off. Everyone was so impressed at how alert and good-humoured she was. I was proud as punch. Ronnie asked me how Mark was.

'Oh, well he's a doting father. He's…em,' I looked around and most of the others had left or were leaving as breaktime was over. I waited for them to go and smiled a farewell before continuing. 'Actually, we've split up, Ronnie. I haven't really told anyone yet, only his parents and my brother. I haven't even told my own mother yet.'

Ronnie was quiet and had a disbelieving look in his eye. 'Wow,' he said. 'I wasn't expecting you to say that. I thought you might be getting married or something by now.'

'Yeah,' I agreed. 'I think most people would assume that, but no, we just weren't right for each other. We're still living together and co-parenting, but I'm not sure how long we'll continue to do that. This little one has taken up all our time and we just haven't had a conversation yet about how the future of our family unit will look.'

'Wow, I'm just so surprised by all of this, Emma. Really, what a shocker! I hope you're okay. Are you okay?' He looked genuinely concerned.

'Yes, yes I think I am. Thanks for asking,' I smiled, full of gratitude.

Later that day, when I got home, I realised I should start planning for the future. Thoughts of leaving Niamh and returning to the library filled me with dread. Even though I loved my job, I really couldn't imagine leaving my tiny young baby for an eight-hour shift, five days a week. I confronted Mark when he got home from work to see what he thought.

'My parents can mind her for one or two days, so we'd just need a childminder for the other three days. Let's look it up. There must be plenty of places around here.' So, we did. In fact that's all we did for the following week and we couldn't find anyone willing to take on a new baby. The local creche only minded children from one year plus and most of the childminders were full up or only admitting afterschoolers. We started panicking when we realised how dire the situation was and I was due back in the library in less than three months. The hunt for a local childminder consumed us until one day I did the maths and came up with a plan.

'I'll mind children here, in the house! If it's that hard for us to find childcare, others must be struggling too. I've looked it up and I can start a course from home and once accredited, I can advertise locally to mind children. I've lots of experience now from the toddler mornings. I feel comfortable working with kids and I'm very organised and…'

'Emma, slow down! What about your job in the library?'

'I know, but I can apply for an extension of my maternity leave. I think I can take an extra sixteen weeks unpaid, so that's enough time to give the childminding a go. By then, I'll know if I'm cut out for it and if not, I'll go back to work. Plus, it gives us extra time to find someone to look after Niamh.'

'And what if you are cut out for it? What then? Would you leave your job?'

'No, not right away. I could apply for a career break, but I'd cross that bridge when…' All of a sudden, his expression changed and he started to look uncomfortable.

'What is it? What's wrong?' I asked.

'Oh, it's just, well, I suppose there'll never be a right time to tell you, but…' He shifted from foot to foot nervously. 'You see, em, well, I've met someone.'

'What?' I could feel myself going pale with shock. 'When? How?'

'At work. I work alongside her and we've always gotten on well. We go for breaks together and she, eh…she just broke up with her long-term boyfriend a few months ago and then I shared our story with her and we've, well, we've realised that maybe all of it happened for a reason. I mean, we've always gotten along, but we've never been single before at the same time. And now, we want to make a go of it. We're starting to make plans.'

'Oh. Oh, I see. That was fast,' I acknowledged.

'YOU broke up with me, Emma. This was all your doing.'

'I know,' I said. 'And I don't regret it.'

His eyes widened. I could tell he was surprised by my newfound confidence.

'So, what sort of plans are you making?' I asked.

'She's got a house, a two-bed duplex in the city centre, near the bank and she, well, she hates living by herself. She's always had company up until about three months ago. She invited me to stay whenever, so…' He trailed off.

'Are you moving in together?' I asked. 'I need to know what you're planning, Mark. It affects me and my future plans too.'

'I know, that's why I'm telling you now. If you're planning to start a childcare business from this house, how are you going to afford a mortgage by yourself? I'm proposing that we sell it by the end of the year. We'll get back what we paid for it and then you can buy a smaller place and I'll move in with Diane for now. It makes sense, financially speaking. Of course, we'll have to work out a timetable for Niamh. I was thinking, three days one week and four the next. Something like that. I was hoping you'd move somewhere near me and Diane so…'

'Stop! Stop! This is too much for me right now. It's like you've got it all planned out. I didn't know I'd be losing the house so soon. I didn't think you'd be moving out. She's only three months old.'

'I know. It's just things are moving fast with me and Diane. We've known each other for years, so it's just… Well, when you know, you know.'

That gave me pause for thought. 'So, em, what age is Diane?' I queried.

'She's thirty-four.' He looked up, almost guiltily.

'Hmmm.' Childbearing age I noted. I knew straight away that was why things were moving fast. Niamh started crying then, so I went to feed her.

Oh no, I panicked, internally. What have I done? I'm losing the family home we bought for

Niamh with the garden and the playroom and the proximity to schools and preschools. Oh no, what have I done? Now I was going to have to buy a little poky apartment and lug a buggy up two flights of stairs and be bus bound with no parking space for my car. Oh no, have I just seriously messed up my daughter's future? I began to sob and Niamh joined in. We cuddled and cried together. She felt it too. We were losing our home and all my plans to work from home and start a childcare business. All those plans I'd made in my head. How naive of me to think it would just work out. How naive! As if dreams could come true for someone as insignificant as me. Stupid, silly me…

Chapter Twenty Four

There was nothing left for me to do. Nothing I could think of. Nothing that would save me. Nothing now, only my mother. She could be the answer to my woes. She was the only one who could safeguard my future and that of my baby's.

But I knew she wouldn't willingly help me out of the goodness of her heart. I would have to beg. And I was prepared to do just that. If it meant being able to hold on to my house and set up a business from home and not have to leave Niamh for eight hours a day to go to work, I would do it. I would get down on my knees and BEG!

The nurses told me she had settled into the nursing home. She didn't make enough progress in the step-down facility in order to be released back into independent living. As I'd just recently given birth and was unavailable for meetings and calls, my brother flew home from England to deal with her transition. He bore the wrath that I would have received had I been more available. The good thing, and we both agreed on this, was that Alan would be able to escape her protests by flying back to the UK. And, by the time I was fit and able to visit her, he had taken all of the blame for the nursing home placement and told my mother that I knew nothing about it, as he hadn't wanted to disturb me in my initial few weeks with Niamh. There wasn't actually a shred of truth in any of it, of course. He'd been on the phone to me every day asking for advice with form filling and meetings with doctors and social workers etc. In the three weeks he was home, he achieved a lot and got her transferred into a nursing home, where she would receive the 24-hour care that she urgently required.

This was going to be my first visit with her since Niamh was born. I'd only spoken with her on the phone up to now. I decided to bring Niamh. I supposed it was about time my mother met her first and only grandchild. I rang ahead to let the nurses know I was coming.

She was sitting out in the day room when I arrived with Niamh asleep in the buggy. The nurses and care staff oohed and ahhed over the sight of a newborn sleeping baby. My mother nodded, but didn't smile. She leaned her head over slightly to peep in and nodded again. I guessed that was her way of saying congratulations or something. For a moment, I froze and wondered if I was doing the right thing. She really seemed to despise me of late. Her attitude towards me worsened as soon as I met Mark. She didn't like that I'd found someone—someone that could potentially make me happy.

I looked around, but there were too many admiring faces present for me to turn and do a runner, so I sat down.

'This place seems lovely! How have you been settling in?' I asked, trying to sound upbeat.

'Hmmm.' She nodded.

'Oh, that's wonderful!' I fake beamed. I was going to have to channel some insincerity, but I didn't feel bad about it. I was doing it for Niamh, for her future.

'We walked through the gardens from the carpark. The grounds are spectacular, so many flowers!' I exclaimed.

'Mmmhmm.' She wasn't giving me much.

'Alan got back safely to the UK,' I reassured her.

'I'm sure he did.' She scowled. 'Couldn't wait to see the back of me. He dumped me in here and ran away. After everything I did for him. No thanks I get, no thanks at all.'

'I, em, I think he thought he was doing right by you. The hospital said you were unfit for discharge and you needed twenty-four-hour care. I mean, he had no choice really.'

'I knew you'd take his side,' she said.

'I'm not taking sides,' I offered. A care attendant approached to offer me tea and biscuits, but I declined. I had a lot of work to do.

'I need to tell you something,' I said. She looked towards me and we made eye contact. 'I broke up with Mark,' I just blurted it out. There was a short pause and I do believe I noticed the corners of her mouth turning slightly upwards.

'So, he left you then, did he? I never liked him.'

'Oh? Oh no, I left him. I broke up with him,' I tried to be frank with her.

She smirked. 'I knew he wasn't to be trusted. Well…has he found someone else?'

'That's not important,' I said, meaning business. 'I have a proposal for you. I need you to listen carefully. Can you do that?' She nodded, wide-eyed and eager for new, juicy information.

'He's moving out,' I said. 'And I want to stay in our house with Niamh. I don't want to sell it. I have plans to open up a business from home. I'm going to take a career break from the library and give it a go, but I need to buy him out.'

She looked at me with a confused expression as if she wasn't expecting any of this. In fairness, she'd never heard me talking like this before. She'd never heard me expressing my wishes. I continued.

'I want to ask you for my inheritance now so I can buy him out and only pay the mortgage for my half of the house. The money from Dad, the money he left to us and you never gave it to us. I'm owed that. And I was thinking if you sold your house, you could divide the proceeds between me and Alan and from that money, we would pay your nursing home fees. That way, you'd have security and I could buy Mark out. Who knows, maybe Alan would return to Ireland if he thought he'd have enough to put down a deposit for an apartment? What do you think?'

Her expression darkened and she narrowed her eyes. 'You're trying to rob me! You two are in cahoots. He threw me in here and now you're trying to take my house and my money! What kind of people have I raised?' She looked seriously angry. I looked around and realised we'd have to keep our voices down. Some of the staff looked a little uncomfortable, as if they weren't sure whether to intervene or not. I asked if I could take my mother to her room and they obliged. She had a lovely, clean, spacious room and I noticed Alan had hung a framed photo of him and Sophie and one of me and him on the wall opposite her bed.

'This room is beautiful!' I acknowledged. 'So much space and…'

'Space for a wheelchair!' she snapped. 'Because I'll be in one for the rest of my life at this rate and I'll die in this room!'

'Mother! Don't be so negative! Of course you'll walk again. No one has said you won't ever walk again. You'll just need to be supported and it's going to take time, but you will. You WILL walk again! I'm sure of it!'

'Ah, what do you care anyway? You have your own family now, your own plans and you only want me for my money.'

Ouch. That hurt. It was true what they say—*the truth hurts.*

'You could help me now by providing a beautiful home for your one and only grandchild and ensure she gets the security of a stay-at-home mom to look after her, especially now that her parents have split up.'

'And?' she barked. Oh, of course, that wouldn't be enough for her. I should have known.

'And,' I said, wondering what else I could give her. 'And…we'd come to visit you…regularly. And when you're allowed, we'd take you out, Niamh and I. We could all go to the playground or a restaurant or…'

'Or to mass?' she added.

'Yes, to mass, of course. I'm sure Niamh would like that too.' I was getting desperate. 'And maybe meet up with Bernadette sometime and go shopping. There's lots we could do if I had the security of owning my home and not having to return to full-time employment in the library.'

'What's this…what's this idea you have for a business? What's all that about?'

That stunned me. She'd just asked me a question! About me! And, MY plans! This was going better than I thought it would!

'There's a shortage of childcare options so I'm going to set up a childcare service from my house. I've done tons of research and there's a huge demand for childcare, so I was hoping to offer a daycare service for toddlers, preschoolers and after-schoolers, depending on demand. I could get fully insured to mind between six to eight children depending on their ages, and if I went for mostly school-going children I'd have my mornings free with Niamh from nine until two pm. I could prepare the meals, organise activities and take Niamh out to the toddler mornings in the library and…'

'And bring her here to visit me.'

'Oh. Yes, we could do that. I don't see why not.' Max one morning a week, I thought to myself. I'm not bringing Niamh to an old folks home every day. Maybe once during the week and an afternoon out at the weekends. That would be enough, for me, and Niamh. I studied her expression. Was she coming round? Was I winning her over?

'Are you sure Mark left you?' she asked out of the blue.

'No, I told you, I left him. Why?'

'Is it him? Did he put you up to this? I wouldn't put it past a banker to try to rob from an elderly person and I never trusted him. Never!'

I sat back. Niamh stirred in the buggy so I rocked it gently back and forth.

'Have you been listening to anything I said? I'm looking towards the future, trying to do what's best for me and Niamh while making sure your needs are met too. This is NOTHING to do with Mark,' I said, choking a little.

'I don't believe you!' she roared.

With that, Niamh cried. She'd need to be fed. I looked at my mother, horrified that she would say something so venomous to me. Tears crept to my eyes, but I didn't have time to let them escape. I had to look after my baby, so I stood up and walked out without saying a word.

*   *   *

Mark rang me later and told me there was a ground floor one-bed apartment for sale near my old apartment block. He reckoned I could afford it if I went back to the library full time when my maternity leave ran out. His mother and Diane offered to mind Niamh, one day each a week. I told him I had to go and hung up. I fell back on the couch. I could feel Niamh slipping away from me. Mark could offer childcare, loving grandparents, and a house with a garden. He also had a partner and most likely would be in a position to bestow siblings to her in the not too distant future.

And what did I have? The prospect of a one-bedroomed apartment with no garden, no chance of siblings, no partner, no family nearby, a toxic grandmother and a mother who had to work a forty-hour week. This meant I'd only see her three nights a week at bedtime and every other weekend because I'd have to share her with Mark. This was awful. The worst possible outcome. I finally let the tears out and they came in streams. I cried that parenthood was going to be a battle from the start. I cried at how naive I was to let Mark go. I cried at how little time I'd get to spend with my daughter. And, I cried for Niamh being forced to grow up in a broken home, shared between two people with completely different agendas. I cried for all of that. And I remembered the hateful way my mother looked at me earlier and I cried about that. Maybe she was right. Right all along. She treated me like I was nothing, because I was nothing. Look at what a mess I'd made of everything. I cried some more and Niamh joined in. We cried and cuddled together on the couch that I'd soon have to sell or leave behind. There was no way it would fit into a one-bed apartment.

Chapter Twenty Five

Mark rang the next morning to ask if he could help me with the sale of our house and submitting an offer for the apartment.

'An offer?' I queried. 'But I haven't even viewed it yet!' It could have been neglected by its former occupants for all I knew. It was on the other side of the complex where my old apartment was, so I had no idea who'd lived there.

'I have, Emma. It's pristine. You'd love it! It's got a south-facing terrace and has recently been renovated throughout. I wouldn't be pushing it if I didn't think it was perfect for you and Niamh.'

'Oh,' I said, taken aback. He had all the research done. He was a fast mover when it came to property transactions. I should have remembered how quickly we acquired this house and sold my old apartment. This was Mark's area of expertise it seemed.

'I'd, em, I'd like to see it for myself first, okay?'

'Sure, I understand. There's a viewing today at three o'clock. You can drop Niamh off with my mother if you don't want to bring her.'

'No, no, that's okay. I'd like to bring her along to what might be her future home.'

'Okay, it's just my mother is only a stone's throw away from it and myself and Diane are within walking distance.'

'I know, I know. It would suit you down to the ground if this works out. I understand.'

'No, Emma. I didn't mean it like that. It would suit you too. The library is only four stops away on the bus and it's a nice little community around there...'

'Okay, okay, Mark. I'll go to see it today.'

As soon as I hung up, the phone rang again. I wondered if it was Mark telling me he'd closed the deal. It wouldn't surprise me. But it wasn't him. It was my old pal Ronnie.

'Hey Emma, just checking in. How are you? How's Niamh?'

'Hi Ronnie. It's, em, well, to be honest, things aren't great.'

'Oh no, are you okay?'

'Yes, but I have to sell our house. Mark has met someone and he wants to sell his share. I can't afford to buy him out so…'

'Oh, I'm sorry about that.'

'Me too. I'm devastated.'

'What are you going to do?' he asked.

'Mark's been looking at apartments for us. He found one that's close to his mother and near where he now lives with his new girlfriend.'

'Wow, he's a fast mover!'

I chuckled. 'I know! Too fast for me. Everything is happening too fast. It's actually in the same complex as my old apartment. The adjoining one.'

'Oh, well, at least you're familiar with the area,' he offered, trying to see the positives.

'Yeah, I know. It's just I'm going to miss this house, this space, and well, I had plans to set up a childcare business from here.'

'You did? Aren't you coming back to the library after your maternity leave?' I detected some alarm in his voice.

'I am now, but I had hoped to take a career break and see if I could become a childminder. Work from home, you know? So I wouldn't have to leave Niamh in a creche or something, but now…well, I suppose that's not going to happen now.'

'Oh, I'm so sorry. I'd be sad if you didn't return to the library, but you're amazing with kids and you have the experience of the toddler mornings and kids' activities. You would have made a success of a childcare business. I know you would!'

Okay, that just made me want to burst into tears. He had such faith in me. It reminded me of Patricia.

'I, em, I have to go, Ronnie,' I choked.

'Oh, okay, but Emma, before you go…'

'Yes?'

'Can I, em, can I? Would it be okay if I called over sometime? You sound lonely and down.'

The tears came, but I spoke through them. 'Yes, Ronnie, that would be okay.'

* * *

Every time Niamh napped, I began tidying and scrubbing to get the house ready for viewings. Knowing Mark, he'd have it on the market within days. I went to view the apartment and as Mark said, it was very well kept, but I just couldn't imagine living there with Niamh. I couldn't put my finger on it. I liked it, but my stomach knotted when I thought about raising a child there. It would suit a single person or a retired person better, not a single mother and her baby. Anyway, I told Mark to go ahead with a bid. I wasn't in a position to refuse his offer of help. I wouldn't have much time to go to other viewings and probably wouldn't find anywhere as suitable.

The next day, as Niamh napped and I was scrubbing toilets, my phone rang. It was the nursing home.

'Emma, your mother tried to get out of bed during the night and had a little fall. She's okay, don't worry.'

'Oh God, I...'

'She's stable. She just sustained a sprained ankle and a little more damage to her wrist, so it will set her back a bit. She, em, she's been trying to assert her independence of late. You know, taking risks.'

'What do you mean?' I asked.

'Well, she's refusing to ring the bell for assistance. She's trying to stand up by herself, exerting pressure on her wrist. She even tried to rob a rollator from another patient, saying she needed it to practice her walking.'

'Oh, I'm sorry. I'll try to have a word with her,' I said, a little mortified.

'Yes, she's been asking for you.'

'She has?' My heart leapt.

'Yes, when she fell, she was calling your name. We had her assessed by the doctor and he suggested she should rest. She kept asking, 'Where's Emma? Where's Niamh?'

'She said Niamh's name? Are you sure?' I didn't think she'd listened to me when I told her my baby's name. She remained neutral, expressing neither like nor dislike for my choice of name.

'Yes, I'm sure. I was there. Do you think you could come by to see her today? I think it might cheer her up.'

Me? Cheer my mother up? That sounded unlikely as hell, but I agreed to try anyway.

When I arrived, she was just waking up from her nap.

'Hi!' I said, holding Niamh in my arms. 'How are you? I heard you fell.'

She perked up and a tiny smile escaped her lips when she saw Niamh in her yellow babygrow, nuzzled against my neck. The glimmer in her eye gave me hope, and I smiled too. I moved closer.

'Would you like to hold her?' I asked.

'Set her down here,' she said. I placed Niamh on her lap with her head resting against her good arm. Niamh didn't whimper, just made some cute gurgling noises. My mother looked down at her and caught her leg with her good hand. She stroked it tenderly. I stood back, not expecting this at all. Tears blinded me, so I looked away. Then, she spoke.

'I'll do it,' she said.

'Do what?' I asked.

'I'll give you the money to buy out Mark.'

'You will?' I exclaimed. 'But why? What changed?'

'Alan rang and reminded me I was nearing death and I should get to know my grandchild before it was too late.'

'He did? He said that?'

'One of the nurses informed him that she saw you storming out, so I had to tell him what happened.'

'And what did he say?' Thank you Nurse Whoever, I acknowledged in my head.

'He said he wouldn't ring me or visit me ever again until I made amends with you. So, that's what I'm doing now. You can sell the house and give Alan his share and I suppose I'll just have to trust that you'll keep up payment for the nursing home and keep your promise of weekly visits.' Then, she added, 'With Niamh.'

I liked that she added that. It made me smile. And I didn't care about her motivations, I was just beyond ecstatic that my dreams of owning my house and starting a business with Niamh close to me might actually come true.

'Thank you,' I sobbed. 'Thank y…'

'Take her back,' she said abruptly. 'She has a dirty nappy.'

'Gladly,' I smiled and hugged Niamh with her stinky bottom close to my chest.

*   *   *

Mark should have been happy for me, but he wasn't. He tried to put me off, telling me I was taking a huge risk going into business by myself and the mortgage repayments were huge for just one person. But I knew he was trying to dissuade me because Diane's house was farther away than he'd like and his parents were on the other side of town.

Alan, on the other hand, was over the moon. He booked a flight to come home and visit our mother, but really to help me get ready to turn my house into a child friendly hub. He was pretty handy with DIY and assured me he'd install the new swingset in the back garden, together with the child locks and stair gate. I would order the playhouse and mini desks and everything else I needed to brighten up the house and make it welcoming for prospective clients. This was a well-to-do area and I knew everything I offered would have to be of an exemplary high standard.

As soon as I stuck a note up on the local supermarket's notice board, the phone didn't stop ringing. I'd been right about the high demand. I knew I'd have no problem filling my eight spots, as soon as my childminding licence arrived in the post.

*　　*　　*

Mark brought legal documents over for me to sign to divide the care of Niamh. We had nothing formal drawn up, up to now. I was glad Alan was home to support me with signing the forms. We pledged that each of us would take Niamh every second weekend and then share her during the week. I would have her three days and she'd be minded by Mark's mum two days a week. Mark would stay with his parents on those two evenings. I swallowed my tears and tried to be brave while signing the forms. After all, it had been my choice to break up with Mark and I had to live with the consequences.

Alan flew back to the UK and Mark came over after work that Friday evening to collect Niamh for her first official weekend with Daddy. Up to now, before the legalities were drawn up, we had shared her at the weekends to suit the fact that I was breastfeeding, but now that we had a formal agreement, Mark was going to keep her until Sunday night.

I had everything ready and enough bottles to see them through until the next day. I'd express some milk in the morning and he said he'd collect those bottles in the afternoon. As soon as the front door was closed, I collapsed on the floor behind it. I wept my heart out until I had no tears left. I picked myself up and made some tea and toast. I needed some comfort and the smell of toast provided that. I brought it into the sitting room and flicked through the channels. I couldn't concentrate, but the hot tea made me feel a little better, more human. Then, I spilled a little by accident when the doorbell frightened the life out of me.

Oh no, what did I forget? I'd put in enough vests, hadn't I? Her 'blanky' was tucked in beside her. Her blue elephant teddy...did I pack that one? He'd hardly come back for that, would he? I opened the door, but to my surprise it wasn't Mark and Niamh. It was Ronnie.

'Oh my God, Ronnie! What a surprise!' I exclaimed.

'Hi Emma, is this a good time?' he asked with such warmth in his eyes that I hadn't previously noticed.

'A good time? As good as any!' I laughed. 'It's my first weekend without Niamh, so I'm on my own,' I told him.

'Oh gosh, are you okay? You've been crying, haven't you?'

I nodded, feeling my puffy eyes. Then I noticed he was standing with his hands behind his back. 'What's that you're hiding, Ronnie?' I asked.

'Well, funny you should ask,' he smiled. 'I think the lady is in need of some cheering up. And d'you know what? I've got just the thing!' he grinned.

I broke out laughing. 'What the heck are you talking about?'

'Din, din, din…drum roll, please!' he announced.

I wondered if he was about to shove powdery, pollen-filled lilies in my face like Mark had once done. Or push a bunch of thorny roses into my arms for me to prick my finger on. Again, as Mark had once done.

But he didn't. He wasn't hiding flowers behind his back at all.

I mimed a drum roll to humour him, mid laughter.

'Louder, please,' he insisted, raising his eyebrows. 'I urgently require you to take your responsibility as Prima Drum Roller seriously!' I upped the ante on my ridiculous attempt at a drumming sound, safe in the knowledge that I wouldn't be waking Niamh, because she wasn't here.

Finally, when our shared drumbeat reached its crescendo, Ronnie theatrically revealed what he was hiding behind his back.

My curiosity was quenched as he majestically unveiled his ukulele.

Epilogue

I finally connected with my mother's friend Bernadette, who lived in the same neighbourhood as me. She often accompanied me to visit my mother in the nursing home and brought with her some lightness and humour on the days when Angela was grouchy.

Bernadette was so enthusiastic and impressed with my colourful set-up for the kids that she promptly named my house *Emma's House of Fun*. It became known locally as that and my waiting list of prospective clients grew and grew. I was managing to live comfortably, afford my monthly mortgage repayment and mind Niamh full-time.

It warmed my heart to see my mother smile at Niamh. She seemed to smile more now as she got older and a little more confused. Her needs were being met and she was safe in the nursing home and I think we both knew she was in the right place, although only one of us admitted it. She talked less and less of the money Alan and myself '*owed*' her because Niamh's cute, babyish antics distracted her to no end. Bingo, board games and sing-songs were her social life now and she even made a few friends with the other elderly ladies in her section. The local priest visited every Sunday to say mass, so that was the highlight of her week. Niamh and myself had to be content with second place.

Mark's mum dropped a day minding Niamh, when the twins were born. I was delighted for Mark and Diane and hugely impressed that they managed to create a family of four after only getting together one year ago. My main source of delight stemmed from the fact that Mark rescinded part of our legal agreement and I got to spend more time with Niamh. She only spent every second weekend with him and one afternoon with his parents.

I could live with that. Besides, I was never lonely. There was always loads to do, like cleaning, cooking and organising the following week's activities for the kids. I didn't bear the burden alone, though. Ronnie dropped over resources from the library when required. He also stayed with me every second weekend when Niamh was with Mark and there was a looming sense of danger that I might perhaps get lonely.

And then I gave him the key, because I realised after a few months of the resumption of our friendship that his presence in my life was urgently required.

The End

NOTE FROM THE AUTHOR

Many thanks for taking the time to read my book. If you enjoyed it, I'd be very grateful if you would leave a review ;-)

If you'd like to connect, you can reach me at:
rachelraffertybooks@gmail.com

And I reveal juicy gossip about my characters, hidden scenes and stories of my writing life in Ireland as a busy working mom in *Rachel's Dublin Diaries*. Just click:
rachelrafferty.com/diary

ACKNOWLEDGEMENT

Huge thanks to my wonderful family for knowing
and understanding that sometimes I just have to
drop everything and write.

OTHER BOOKS BY RACHEL RAFFERTY

Perfectly Reasonable
Abundantly Clear
Somewhat Satisfactory

Printed in Great Britain
by Amazon

18097517R00140